I0645401

KING DAYVID

TY MARSHALL

KING DAYVID

Copyright © 2020 by Ty Marshall.

Marshall House Media™ and all associated logos are trademarks of Marshall House Media LLC.

All rights reserved. Printed in the United States of America. No part of this book may be used or reproduced in any manner whatsoever without written permission except in the case of brief quotations em- bodied in critical articles or reviews.
This book is a work of fiction. Names, characters, businesses, organiza tions, places, events and incidents either are the product of the author's imagination or are used fictitiously. Any resemblance to actual persons, living or dead, events, or locales is entirely coincidental.

For information contact :
MarshallHouseMedia@gmail.com

http://www.tymarshallbooks.com

Book Cover design by Nicole Watts
ISBN: 978-0-9984419-8-6

First Edition: May 2020

10 9 8 7 6 5 4 3 2 1

"King Saul envied David before he even became king.

King Saul had the position, but David had the anointing

& power." *-Ty Marshall*

PROLOGUE

"Who am I, O Lord and what is my family that you have brought
me this far?" *-Samuel 7:18*

The lights on the minivan went dark immediately as it bent the corner onto the quiet, secluded street. Slowing to a creep, as it pulled alongside the curb, the minivan finally came to a rest in the middle of the block just before the engine cut off. Positioned in the driver's seat, behind extremely dark tints, sat Dayvid Porter; King Dayvid to the streets. The only male sibling of the infamous Porter clan, that consisted of two younger sisters, Autumn and Fallon, along with his twin sister Rain. Dayvid was the most feared member of the lawless family that had terrorized the state of Maryland for the past five years. They pulled off bank jobs, jewelry heist and robbing every big money hustler in and around the state. Money was his sole motivation and Dayvid didn't mind putting his murder game down to get it. There was no 401k in the Porter's line of work, but as they sat parked in the stolen minivan, Dayvid's eyes were glued across the street at the closest thing to a retirement package.

The Brink's armored truck depot was not just the place where the bullet proof vehicles were parked at night. The building housed a vault that banks and businesses used to store cash and jewelry, and on any given day it could hold a couple million dollars easily.

Rain, as usual, had masterminded the heist, along with Smitty, their consultant and advisor, who enjoyed an illustrious run of his own robbing banks during the 80's. Smitty was a vital piece to their intricate operation. He had gotten the inside scoop on the layout of the building, including camera positions and the number of guards on duty, from a couple disgruntle employees looking to make a nice piece of change off assisting with the heist. The workers would never see their cut though; Dayvid would make sure the both of them disappeared shortly after the heist. He was what Smitty sometimes referred to as a cleaner, the person who got rid of all the loose ends that could connect the Porters to any job they did. The criminal quartet only trusted a select few who weren't blood, everyone else were pawns and viewed as expendable.

Dayvid looked down at his watch, which read *11:50 p.m*; it was almost go time. Friday night was the perfect time to hit the facility, the vault was left open due to the large quantity of money being

moved throughout the night, preparing to replenish the ATM machines around the city of Baltimore. The Porters were the only crew brave enough to attempt such a brash robbery.

"You ready to do this shit?" he asked looking over at his twin sister who sat slumped in the passenger seat checking her weapon.

"Do bears shit in the woods?" Rain sarcastically replied.

"What about you Fallon, you ready? I need you to be focused when we get in this jawn, no bullshittin', no fuck ups," he sternly stated glaring in his rearview mirror at his younger sister in the backseat.

"I know, I got this, I'm not gonna let y'all down," Fallon spoke up trying her best not to sound intimidated by her brother.

Nothing else needed to be said, they all knew what was at stake. If all went as planned, they will be sipping margaritas on the beaches of Mexico this time tomorrow. The three siblings pulled their masks down over their faces and exited the car. Creeping quickly across the street using the darkness as their cover, they pressed up against the wall and waited for the camera on the building to rotate. Dayvid had the timing down of all the cameras they would have to pass on their way through the building. Having rehearsed this dance numerous times in the past few weeks, he felt as though they could have navigated the building blindfolded. Now sure they could move undetected, he pulled out the key provided to him by the employee and slid it into the lock. Rain and Fallon pulled out their guns, crouched down and swiftly moved through the open door with

Dayvid following close behind.

The Porters were stealth in their movements as they made their way through the facility until they reached the staff cafeteria. Slipping inside the break room, they hid out until they heard the bell signaling break time for the security guards on duty. Lying in wait, they subdued each guard that entered the break room, one by one. Making everyone lay face down on the floor, Dayvid held the room at gun point while Rain and Fallon used zip tie cuffs on their hands and feet.

Rain checked the nametags of each employee before snatching a key card off one of the guards and tossing it to Fallon. They were provided with the last name of the guard who was in possession of the key card that would get them into the vault area and so far the information had proven to be right.

Continuing down the hallway until they came to another door that required the swipe, Fallon quickly swiped the access card on the set of keys and waited to hear the door click, signaling it was open. Dayvid put up his hand, using his fingers he silently counted to three. On three the Porters invaded the vault area with their weapons drawn, pointing directly at the four guards in the room. Caught by surprise they had the three men and one woman face down on the floor before they were able to hit the button setting off the alarm or go for their weapons.

"Robbery or homicide, your choice," Dayvid yelled. "Look straight at the floor and put your hands behind your back," he barked out instructions. "If you look at me, I'll blow your fuckin head off, we clear?" he said pressing his shotgun against the back of one of the men's head as his sisters used the zip tie cuffs to restrain the group.

Dayvid walked over to the operating station and pressed a button on the switchboard. He watched on the closed-circuit monitor as the gate opened and a white cargo van sped through. The three siblings waited as the van backed up to the dock and came to a stop. When the two doors flew open, their baby sister Autumn stood there waiting to begin loading the empty van up with cash.

The four of them moved like a well-oiled machine making quick work of the vault. They grabbed close to 3 million in cash and jewelry in seven minutes, not wanting to stay too long; knowing that trucks would begin pulling up soon to get loaded for their routes.

"Time," Rain shouted just as Fallon emerged from a back room holding the security tapes in her hands.

"Let's go!" Dayvid shouted jumping in the back of the van as Rain and Fallon followed. He slammed the doors shut as Autumn started up the engine and peeled off.

A short time later Autumn pulled the cargo van into a garage a few miles away from the armored truck depot. It was one of the many stash spots the Porters had in and around the city of Baltimore. They quickly exited the van and began transferring the take from the van into one of the two waiting cars. The only car they didn't put money in was the car Dayvid was driving.

"Aiight y'all know the plan. Straight to the safe house, no stops," he said to his sisters. "I'ma go tie up these loose ends," he said cocking his gun. "And I'll be right there. Then we outta here first thing tomorrow." Dayvid kissed Autumn and Fallon on the forehead like usual.

"Mexico here we come," Fallon said with a smile as she slapped five celebrating with her baby sister, almost able to hear the waves slamming against the beach and feeling the sun on her beautiful brown skin.

"I can't wait," Autumn sighed relieved at the thought of putting the life behind her and enjoying a normal life with her siblings for a change.

"Be safe D," Rain said not yet ready to celebrate like her younger sisters.

"C'mon slim, you already know," he dapped Rain up trying to reassure her, but knew it would do nothing to ease her fears. Dayvid knew Rain would be pacing back and forth at the safe house until he walked through the door. That was how she was when it came to her siblings.

"Straight to the safe house," he repeated once more as he pulled the black Challenger out the garage.

* * *

"Yo, I gotta go hit Smitty off before we leave," Rain said as she picked her gun up off the table and put it in her waist.

"Damn you didn't handle that earlier?" Dayvid asked as he took a gulp of champagne.

"Nah, I got too busy. I was trying to get to the safe house, and I forgot to stop by his place." Rain walked over to the smallest bag that contained close to one hundred thousand dollars in it and threw it over her shoulder.

"You want me to roll with you?" he asked placing his glass down on the table.

"Nah, I'm good. Y'all do y'all thing and I'll be back later. Save me some champagne too nigga," Rain said as she finished off her glass, dapped her brother up and headed for the back door.

"Rain," Dayvid called out. "Smitty's and back, no extra shit," knowing she would probably stop by her girlfriend Laura's house no matter what he said.

Rain just nodded her head and smiled before disappearing out the door.

Dayvid pick up the lit blunt from the ashtray, taking a long pull, filling his lungs with OG Kush then slowly exhaled the smoke. He rose to his feet snatching the open bottle of champagne off the table before walking over to the fireplace. Retrieving his clothes from the robbery off the floor, he tossed all the articles of clothing into the burning fire, including the ski mask. Seeing the clothes burning seemed to bring a calming feeling over him as he took another hit of the weed. For as long as he could remember money, murder, and mayhem had consumed his every thought, he had never second guessed it. Protect and provide, Dayvid was the best at both when it came to his siblings. Maybe a little too good if you asked Fallon and Autumn. The two of them felt that he could be overprotective at times, even more than Rain. His overbearing ways forced them to keep things from him when it came to certain parts of their lives, mainly their love lives. The loss of their parents, especially their mother, had affected Dayvid more than any of the other Porter siblings. He was the closest to Remy and had become extremely reticent after her death; internalizing the pain and vowing to never let anything happen to someone he loved again. That was why he behaved the way he did with his sisters.

Fallon knew this all too well after choosing Linx over her siblings, only to have to return with her tail between her legs. While her two sisters were happy to have her back in the fold and welcomed her with open arms, Dayvid had been slow to come around. He had shown a callous indifference towards Fallon since her return and it had affected the relationship negatively. He felt a deep sense of betrayal and hurt by her actions, after all Autumn and Fallon's well-being was the driving force behind most of the risk, he and Rain had taken over the years. So, her defection was a spit in his face. Deep in his thoughts, while staring into the burning fire, he hadn't even noticed Fallon making her way across the room, until she was only a few feet from him. The sound of her heels clicking on the hardwood floor made him turn to face her.

"Hey D," she said trying to work up the nerve to say what was on her mind.

Dayvid's strong personality and demeanor could be very intimidating to most, he always said less than necessary which left a bit of mystery about him. He stood over six feet tall with a slim but solid built frame and piercing eyes with a tattoo tear under one of them. The lightest of all the Porters, Dayvid was extremely handsome, his light skin complexion and deep-dish waves on his fade made him appear more Puerto Rican than black. His neck was fully covered in tattoos, giving him a grimy edge but his flawless set of teeth and deep dimples gave him undeniable sex appeal and boyish charm. His face remained emotionless as he nodded his head in response to her greeting and blew out a cloud smoke from the side of his mouth.

Still not sure if her timing was right, Fallon decided to take the opportunity to clear the air between the two of them once and for all. "I know you feel a way about me Dayvid and I've apologized many times, but it seems like you refuse to forgive me. I don't know what it is that you want from me, but I just want things between us to go back to the way they were." Fallon stared at him looking for any reaction but received none.

Dayvid was a hard nut to crack and even harder to read, a man of few words who preferred to let his actions speak for him. That worked in the streets but frustrated those closest to him. For years he would shut down refusing to share his thoughts with anybody, not even his twin. Dayvid was truly an alpha male, leader of the Porter pack and he took his role as big brother deathly serious. There was a natural bond between him and Autumn, it was the big brother, baby sister thing. No matter how old she got he will always see her as the little girl jumping up and down on his bed begging him to take her to the candy lady in the neighborhood. But Dayvid's feelings for Fallon went deeper than anyone knew. Fallon was the mirror image of their mother, Remy, the woman who Dayvid's love for bordered on worship. He had always loved Fallon slightly more than the rest because of that. Her defection from the family hit him hard and although she was back, he remained guarded not willing to allow her all the way back in his heart.

"I feel like you love me less and that hurts. I've always respected what you do and have done for all of us, but you're my brother not my father and I'm not a little girl anymore. The things I've done and seen out in these streets, most times at your behest, is more than most people see in a lifetime. And for the most part I've done them all without question. How long will you hold my one mistake over my head?" she wanted to know.

Dayvid rubbed his hand over his neatly groomed facial hair. He knew Fallon had a valid point, he had placed her in harm's way plenty of times, using her intoxicating beauty like a weapon, sending her at many of their unsuspecting victims. She would have never come in contact with the bitch nigga, Linx, if it wasn't for him trying to line the nigga up as a mark. Maybe it was the weed and liquor or the fact that they had just accomplished what so many before them had failed to do; retire on their own terms at the top of the game. But after hearing her words, Dayvid decided that Fallon had more than redeemed herself and he was just being a stubborn hard ass with his sister.

"You right Fallon," he said causing her eyes to widen in shock. "I've been too hard on you and you don't deserve that. Everyone is entitled to make mistakes but you my blood, my lil' sis, not some nigga in the street."

"Hold up, did you just say I was right?" Fallon said jokingly still a little shocked.

"Yeah, don't make me regret it tho slim," he said flashing a smile turning his normally mean mug handsome.

Fallon just stared at him. She had almost forgotten how good looking her brother was. She had grown so accustomed to his scowl, that the sight of his deep dimples made her smile. "I love you D," she said wrapping her arms around his neck and squeezing him tight relieved that the tension between them was gone.

"I love you too sis," he said hugging her back and kissing her on the forehead. "Porters under God."

"Porters under God," she replied before pulling back and lifting her glass in the air to meet the bottle he was holding. They toasted then both took big gulps.

BAM! BAM! BAM!

Dayvid saw Fallon's face immediately flood with fear looking as if she had just seen a ghost. The thunderous sound and terrifying look on her face let Dayvid know exactly what was happening. *The fuckin' boys,* he thought to himself. But he wasn't going down without a fight though, always vowing he would hold court in the streets before he spent a day in jail. He had done so much, that he knew if and when they came for him and his siblings, they would never see another free day alive. *How the fuck is this happening? Why now?* he asked himself as his mind raced and things seemed to go in slow motion. Before he could reach for his gun sitting on the table, where he and Rain had sat minutes earlier, there was another loud noise followed by a bright flash. Dayvid felt his body jerk forward and crash violently to the hardwood floor sending a bone chilling pain through his body. Attempting to get to his feet, he was met with a powerful stomp from a large boot to the back, forcing him back onto his stomach.

"Arrgh," Dayvid grunted still never dropping the blunt that was dangling out of his mouth.

"Police! Let me see your fucking hands! Everybody let me see your fucking hands! Nobody fucking move!" one of the officers roared out instructions, while pointing his assault rifle at Dayvid as the ATF swarmed the safe house.

"Dayvid!" Autumn cried out as an officer threw her face down on the table, spilling a bottle of champagne over the piles of cash in the process.

"Listen to me," Dayvid demanded. "Nobody say shit to these ma'fuckas. No matter what they say, they don't know shit. So, don't fall for it. Keep ya'll fuckin' lips shut tight," he concluded staring directly at Fallon. She nodded her head and nothing else needed to be said.

"Shut the fuck up," the officer barked as he dropped a knee into Dayvid's back, causing the blunt to fall out his mouth as another man cuffed him.

"Stand him up," shouted the vanilla gorilla looking officer with the crew cut. It was clear by the way he strutted into the room that he was the one in charge.

Dayvid watched as the man walked over to him and got right into his face. He could feel his breath on his skin, they were so close their noses were almost touching.

The officer began nodding his head and smiling as he got a look at the tattoo on Dayvid's face. "King Dayvid," he announced sarcastically as if he needed to say the name out loud in order to believe who he had custody. "Oh, I've been waiting a long time for this," he said all breathy as if he was becoming turned on by the capture.

"It's only three of them here, sir," one of the officers informed as he emerged from another room after searching the house.

"Where's your twin sister or should I say twin brother," he joked. "Where's Rain?" he demanded an answer, almost chanting her name.

Dayvid just stared straight ahead and remained silent. He would die a thousand deaths before he compromised his principles as a man and cooperated with the police.

"You ain't got nothing to say?" the white gorilla looking officer quizzed.

In typical Dayvid fashion, he looked down at the floor, then back at the officer before saying, "Hate to see that weed go to waste."

The officer cocked back and landed a thudding blow into Dayvid's stomach knocking the wind out of him. "Get him the hell outta here," the frustrated man yelled.

1

"Then Bathsheba bowed with her face to the earth, and did reverence to the king, and said, "Let my lord King David live forever." -*1 King 1:31*

Nova James opened the front door of her apartment and picked up the morning edition of the Baltimore Sun. Walking through her spacious living room, charmingly decorated with all white leather furniture and red wine throw pillows, she tossed the paper onto the white and glass coffee table before hurrying into the kitchen to pour her morning coffee. Gliding back into the living room with her freshly brewed decaf in hand, she grabbed the paper off the table and flipped it open. Nova's hands suddenly went limp as she lost grip on the coffee mug sending it crushing to the floor into pieces, spilling hot brown liquid everywhere. Nova felt as if she couldn't breathe reading the headline blazoned across the front page:

3 OF THE INFAMOUS PORTER SIBLINGS IN CUSTODY AFTER RAID ON SAFE HOUSE; RAIN PORTER STILL AT LARGE.

With her hands trembling uncontrollably Nova picked the remote up off the table, clicked on the TV and flipped through the channels until she landed on the local news. It didn't take long for her to see the faces of the Porters plastered on her screen. Tears streamed down her beautiful face leaving a trail on her golden skin as her worst fears were coming to fruition in front of her eyes. Unable to bear it anymore Nova walked to the double glass door that led out to her balcony, pushed them open and stepped out. Staring down at the steady flow of traffic below, the pain she felt in her gut had only been felt by her once before. Instantly, the luxurious apartment with the impeccable view lost all its appeal and her feeling of invulnerability shattered into a pile of guilt. After all, she knew the vast amount of blood that had been spilled for her to sit perched atop of the high rise overlooking the city. But that wasn't the root of her remorse, her regret came from not being able to get the man she loved out the streets before it was too late. Nova turned her face to the heavens hoping for divine intervention.

"Lord, I know what he does, and I know who he is but he's all I have, and I love him," she prayed.

* * *

A Few Weeks Ago

Nova stood in the mirror staring at her reflection. She traced her finger against her collarbone and reflected on everything she had been through over the last ten years. The hurt, the deceit, the lies, all the cover ups and the riding she had done for the man lying in her bed. She looked past her reflection and stared at Dayvid relaxing on her king size bed in nothing but his boxer briefs and a wife beater. Nova's eyes met his as she noticed him studying her every move.

"You know I love you right?" was all he said to her. He knew her very well, better than most, shit better than anyone; he knew what made her tick. Her pain and her strength to stay although she knew all this could be over in the blink of an eye.

"I know," she replied in a soft tired voice.

"Come here," he motioned while moving towards the edge of the bed. "Everything I do, I do for you, I do it for us. You know that, right?" Dayvid asked pulling Nova down on his lap and wrapping his arms around her waist.

There was no one besides his sisters that he loved more than Nova, she was beautiful in every way to him, inside and out. She was five foot seven, one hundred and sixty pounds, thick and curvy. Her skin was a golden complexion and her doe eyes were inviting to any man who met her. Dayvid had been with Nova since the both of them were teenagers. He was the first man she had willingly slept with and the only one she had ever loved. After losing her mom to a heroin overdose at fifteen and her dad never being a part of her life, Dayvid was all she had, and she couldn't fathom the thought of losing him. He knew this and sheltered her because of it. He never wanted to involve her in his criminal ways but knew without a shadow of doubt that she would ride with him for whatever, against whomever. He set her up in a two-bedroom condo in The Palisades of Towson about 20 minutes north of the city of Baltimore and made sure everything she needed was at her grasp. In the beginning she was frustrated, thinking Dayvid had only stashed her miles away so he could do his dirt with the herds of women in the city. Dayvid's reputation spoke for itself, his silent gangster aura and good looks drove women crazy and Nova knew it.

He would always try to ease her worries by telling her, "a real man is supposed to teach you the game, not run it on you."

As time passed, she began to realize it was for her own safety, still she didn't like that Dayvid insisted on accompanying her whenever she wanted to go shopping or go to the grocery store. Back in the day it wasn't like that, she was able to roam freely, but the bigger Dayvid became the more precautions he took. King Dayvid was feared in the streets but that led to more hate and animosity, he was smart enough to know that niggas wouldn't try to go at him but would relish in hurting those he loved. Being the precious jewel that Nova was to him, Dayvid knew he could never recover or forgive himself if anything ever happened to her. She was not only his woman and lover she was his best friend. She was his queen.

"When is all this going to stop Dayvid? I need you. I need you to be free. How am I supposed to think about our future when our present could end at any given moment?" she questioned.

Dayvid noticed the frustration in her tone, he knew it all too well. She was always scared of something bad happening to him. Nova would fidget with her fingers when her mind was racing a million miles per minute. He intertwined his fingers with hers to calm her nerves and lifted her hand, kissing her ring finger, where she had their matching tattoos. She wore a queen of hearts and he wore a king of hearts on his to symbolize their love for one another.

"I ain't going nowhere ma, this is it for us. We in, we out and we done this time," speaking in reference to the one last heist he and his sisters were planning. "This shit is gonna set us straight. I'll never have to step foot in these streets again. You hear me?" he lifted her chin so that she could engage him eye to eye. He needed her to understand his sincerity. Although he told this story once before, Dayvid knew this was it for him and all he wanted to do was make sure his sisters were set up and straight and his girl will forever be good. Nova didn't know but he had plans on making her his wife once they got to Mexico. He wanted to be a family man, settle down, have two or three kids. He often wondered if he would have a set of twins of his own. The thought of it brought a smile across his face, his smile would always make Nova change her attitude about any situation. Dayvid would light up a room with it and his dimples melted any tough façade she tried to put up. It was his best feature though he rarely showed it to anyone but her.

"I love you Dayvid Porter and I plan on loving you for two lifetimes, so you better not be lying," she said returning his smile but trying to still show the seriousness of her words.

"And I'll give my life for you Nova James, twice," he said while pulling her in for a kiss.

They interlocked their tongues passionately and Dayvid picked her up in his arms, carrying her in a fetal positon. His size made her look tiny and her weight was light as a feather for him. Dayvid laid her on the bed gently, pulling her panties down while sporting a boyish grin as he placed her black cotton panties on his head like a hat. Nova giggled at the sight of her sexy modern day outlaw sporting her underwear on his head.

"Yeah, I wear these proudly," he boasted pulling them over his face and inhaled her scent then letting them rest around his neck. "I love how your smell," he continued while biting down on his bottom lip.

Nova immediately knew she was in for a treat, she knew her man and before Dayvid looked to please himself, he reveled in pleasing her body. She spread her legs eagle wide across the bed and Dayvid went head first into her love spot. Licking every crevice of her pussy gently before sucking on her clit hard and vigorously as he took in all her juices. Nova caressed his head enjoying the masterful use of his tongue. She began grinding and riding his face as she gripped his ears like a pair of handlebars. Nova felt her orgasm building and quivered in his grasp until she climaxed in his mouth. Unable to take it anymore, Nova pushed his head away and signaled for him to penetrate her. Dayvid was not only good with his tongue game, he laid a serious pipe and she could not wait to feel him inside of her.

Refusing her offer, Dayvid laid his head on her inner thigh. "Nah, ma it's about you tonight. Let me know when you ready to go again." He knew Nova was feeling a certain way that night and his mission was just to please her as she had done for him by devoting her heart and life to him. He couldn't see himself without her and the thought of ever leaving her out in the world by herself was not an option for him.

* * *

Present Day

Baltimore County Detention Center housed some of the city's most hardened criminals and was one of the largest detention facilities in the United States. It was also one of the most corrupt, where money ruled everything, and jail officials were willing to turn a blind eye to almost anything for a profit. Inmates greased palms of correction officers for access to various things that were available to them on the streets including drugs and cell phones. King Dayvid's reputation was the same behind the wall as it was out in the world. He moved through his unit freely, even amongst hustlers he had leaned on and extorted in the streets. He had the respect of every goon and just the sight of him sparked fear in anyone with the slightest bit of pussy in them. Female officers secretly swooned over him, craving for the opportunity to work on his unit, just to get a glimpse of the man whose name was ringing throughout the entire facility. Dayvid remained stoic and unaffected by all the attention.

Locked in his cell, preforming his daily routine of calisthenics and building up a sweat, Dayvid wasn't in a pleasant mood after finding out he wouldn't be going to court that day. He wasn't concerned about his case so much knowing that the feds had enough evidence to bury the Porters underneath the jail. He merely looked forward to seeing his sisters, needing to lay eyes on them to see how they were holding up. He knew Rain was cut from the same cloth as him and was on the outside doing whatever she had to do to stay free, but his younger sisters were different. Though they were Porters, they weren't cut from the same cloth as him and his twin. Dayvid and Rain was breed for the life they led and took to the streets naturally and seamlessly; Fallon and Autumn were simply along for the ride. Dayvid jumped to his feet and stood in front of the sink in his cell, barely able to see his reflection in the dirty mirror; ironic for a man who had begun to see things clearer as of late.

After years of only caring about the next come up, Dayvid had begun to think long term, something other than the streets. A better life for his younger siblings and a normal life with Nova. Mexico had been the result of his new mind frame, but that plan had been interrupted by the federal government with the help of somebody close to them, that he was sure of it. The thought enraged him more than anything. He took a distinct pleasure in executing rats and had made a good living doing just that for some of the most powerful people up and down the east coast. Now he had his own rodent to deal with and couldn't wait to lay his trap. Dayvid had some niggas in the district he knew would be down to help and was already laying the groundwork to get the word to Rain and them through one of the female officers that was sweet on him. Hearing his cell being cracked, Dayvid turned to see his cellmate entering. The two men hadn't said much to one another while sharing a cell. Dayvid wasn't interested in getting cool with anybody.

"You know a nigga named Shake from down East Bawllmer," his celly questioned in his heavy Baltimore accent, seemingly out the blue.

"I know a lot of niggas slim, I ain't good wit names doe," Dayvid responded. Truth was he knew exactly who Shake was. Him and Rain had hit one of his shipments about a year ago, and then made him cop his own work back.

"That's crazy yo, I just got off the phone with him and he knows you real well," the man challenged.

"Is that right?" Dayvid said rubbing his hand over his goatee. "I think you got some false information, Slim. Cuz if a nigga really knew me—" Dayvid said before hooking off on his cellmate, landing a two-piece flush on the man's jaw, dropping him to his knees. Dayvid kneed him in the face a few times then banged his head into the wall of the cell. Seeing the blood leaking from the man's face, Dayvid let his limp body fall to the floor and stomped him repeatedly until his leg got tired. Dayvid washed the blood off his hand in the cell's sink before grabbing his shirt off his bunk. "Like I said, if a nigga really knew me, he knew you pressing me was gonna get your ass whipped," Dayvid said as he stepped over his cellmate and walked out the cell just in time for chow.

Reaching the bottom of the steps, Dayvid got in line to receive his tray and snatch a seat at one of the tables. He was halfway through his meal when a loud roar from a few inmates near the TV caught his attention. The officer on duty screamed for the men to calm down, but only to be ignored. From his seat Dayvid could see the TV and quickly rose to his feet when he recognized his sisters Rain and Autumn's faces on the screen.

"Yo, turn that up," he instructed one of the other inmates walking up on the men now gathered around the tube.

Dayvid watched as the news showed the aftermath at the courthouse, site of the audacious escape pulled off by Rain and Autumn. It looked like some shit out the Wild West and Dayvid unknowingly held his breath as the reporter reeled off the names of the casualties. Fallon's face hadn't been shown or reported at large like his other two siblings and Dayvid felt a sense of uneasiness. He was finally able to breathe easy after hearing she wasn't among the dead and in fact was still in custody like him. Knowing Rain, the way he did, he knew it wasn't her plan just to free Autumn and she probably assumed they all would be in route to the courthouse that morning. She was probably stressing out now trying to come up with a way to free him and Fallon. While Dayvid took pleasure in knowing two of his sisters were now free, he knew Rain's bold actions had made it that much harder for him and Fallon to escape. Shooting his way out was now off the table, he would have to rely on his intelligence and strength as a strategist if he ever planned on seeing the people he loved again.

Dayvid was brought out of his deep thought by the sound of the door of the unit opening followed by a flood of swat team members entering the unit. Inmates dropped to the floor on their stomachs with their hands stretched out in front of them at the sight of the Turtles, as they were called by the prisoners. Dayvid already knew who they were there for and the smirk on his face needled the group of officers.

"Get the fuck on the ground!" one of them screamed at a defiant Dayvid who stood with his fists clinched refusing to follow orders. "On the ground now!" he repeated.

"Last chance Porter!" another man screamed.

Dayvid refused, hocking up phlegm from his throat and spitting it in the direction of the officers. The glob landed on one of the swat member's face shield, triggering the group to rush Dayvid who stood his ground, throwing a series of punches. His efforts were quickly thwarted. Outnumbered the officers easily pounded him into submission before handcuffing him and carrying him out the unit to the sound of cheers from the other inmates.

After Rain's theatrics, the feds felt Dayvid's power, influence and money would prove too much for the walls of BCDC to contain him. They couldn't afford the embarrassment of another Porter escaping their grasp. The order had come down swiftly; Dayvid was being transferred to the North Branch Correctional Institution, a super-maximum prison located in Cresaptown, near Cumberland.

2

"The Lord laughs at the wicked, for he knows their day is coming."

-Psalm 37:13

September 2006

Dayvid pulled off the exit and merged onto Jessup Road as the sounds of Birdman & Lil' Wayne's "Leather So Soft" pumped through the car. After a few minutes he pulled up to a nice sized house and turned his black '69 SS Camaro into the driveway before cutting off the engine. Smitty's house sat in the middle of a quiet suburban neighborhood about 15 miles south of the city, in Jessup County, perfect for the unassuming advisor of the Porters. The middle aged man was standing in the driveway with his signature straw hat and toothpick hanging from his mouth. Smitty had seamlessly blended into the neighborhood and could regularly be seen outside watering his grass while sharing small talk with his neighbors who were ignorant to his checkered past. A smile crept across his face seeing Dayvid pulling in. He instantly began admiring the classic old school whip Dayvid was pushing.

"Whoo," Smitty said, nodding his head in approval as he walked up on the vintage vehicle getting a closer look. "That's clean right there King," calling Dayvid by the nickname he had christened him with many years ago after witnessing him destroy a neighborhood bully a few years older and twice his size in a fist fight. Smitty was amazed, he had been willing to bet a pocket full of cash that the young Porter had bitten off more than he could chew. But Dayvid's hands proved to be far superior during the altercation and had remained that way over the years. Smitty compared the victory to David's over Goliath in the bible. As the story in the bible told it, David would go on to become king, and Smitty said so would the only male Porter one day. His premonition had been correct, Dayvid Porter was street royalty.

Smitty greeted the young gangster with a pound when he exited the car. "Come on," Smitty waved his hand, signaling for Dayvid to follow him back into the house. "You want something to drink?" he asked once they were inside while offering him a seat on the couch.

"Nah, I'm good. This ain't gonna take that long OG." Dayvid replied choosing to remain standing.

"What's on ya mind then?" Smitty asked plopping down on the

couch.

"You got company?" Dayvid inquired looking around making sure he could speak freely.

Smitty was a handsome older gentleman, straight old school with a slick silver tongue, spitting game with every word. He was known to keep company with many different women and his bed was seldom cold. So it wasn't far-fetched that he would have a female in the house.

"We good, go ahead," he answered in his normal smooth manner.

"Listen I just wanted to stop by and tell you in person that we're gonna pass on that job we talked about last week," Dayvid informed him.

"Whatchu mean you gonna pass on it?" a confused Smitty questioned.

"It's just not a move I think we should make right now, especially since we're undermanned with Fallon off playing house with this nigga Linx. That shit ain't a three-man job."

Clearly bothered by what he was hearing from his young protégé', Smitty leaned back on the couch and took a deep breath while running his hand down the side of his face.

"But peep this, I gotta crew from The District that I could put on it tho. You'll get your same exact cut and won't even have to meet these niggas. I'll take care of all that; even less of a risk for you but the same paper. You can't beat that." Dayvid offered his mentor.

"Fuck you think this is, a temp service or a staffing agency," Smitty snapped. "I'm not looking to do no hiring. We got a system, I set up the jobs, y'all knock em off and everybody goes home happy. Why fuck it up if you don't have to?"

"Outta all due respect, I didn't come here to debate with you. I just came to let you know what it is. If you don't want to do it like that, then cool but we ain't fucking wit it," Dayvid said as he reached in his back pocket and pulled out a thick yellow envelope, sliding it across the table.

"What's this?" Smitty asked.

"25k, outta respect, for the inconvenience." Dayvid explained.

Smitty laughed not even bothering to pick up the envelope. "You gotta be kidding me young nigga. I stand to make at least three times that off this heist," the frustration in his voice evident. "Nah, nah…y'all gonna do this shit, and we gonna get paid, then you can thank me later."

Dayvid stared at his mentor and felt himself getting upset. In all the years of doing business with Smitty they had never backed out of a job but something about this one didn't feel right. Dayvid felt that Smitty should understand him not wanting to do it, but the fact that he hadn't, didn't sit right with him.

"Let me ask you a question…who da fuck you think ya talkin' to?" Dayvid snapped. "You an old nigga with a fucked up leg, who don't understand that his best days are behind him. We don't work for you. We work with you. I decide what my family will and won't do, so it's 25k or it's nothing."

Smitty remained silent, just staring at Dayvid as his chest heaved up and down. He could almost see smoke coming from his flared nostrils, like the young bull he was. Smitty always knew that Dayvid was the alpha male type, he had shown all the traits since a youth but Smitty had been able to will his influence over him a bit when he was younger. But as of late that had become a thing of the past, Dayvid only did what he wanted to do, no ifs, ands or buts. After a few seconds Smitty rose to his feet, letting out a grunt from the pain shooting through his leg. Walking with a faltered step over towards the bar, he poured himself a drink. Dayvid intensely watched with menacing eyes.

"Boy you just like your daddy," Smitty finally spoke after taking a sip of the cognac in his glass, smiling and shaking his head while reminiscing.

Dayvid's face instantly changed, wrinkles formed on his brow, slightly confused by the man's statement. "What you know about my pops to be speaking on him?" He was always under the assumption that Smitty didn't know his parents, only his Aunt Nanny.

"Who ain't know James Porter," Smitty laughed. "Lil nigga I knew your daddy for years," he informed Dayvid. "He worked for me for a while, best getaway drive I ever saw. Your daddy loved cars, just like you. And he could drive the shit out of anything, just like you too. One day he came to me and said he wanted to do his own thing, he was tired of the cut he was getting and wanted a bigger piece. Said he needed more money since he had more mouths to feed, after your baby sister Autumn was born. Told me he was putting his own crew together to pull off a couple of jobs. I understood, no hard feelings, he made a business decision," Smitty concluded.

"Why I ain't never heard this before? Aunt Rachel never said shit about my pops robbing no banks." Dayvid quizzed.

"He never got the chance, he and ya mama died in that car crash about a week later," Smitty said lowering his head in sadness and shaking it from side to side.

"Why you telling me this now, Smitty? What that got to do with this shit?" Dayvid asked quickly trying to change the subject not wanting to think about the tragic accident that claimed his parents' life.

"Just making a point, it's not good to switch up when you gotta good thing going," he said the whole time looking into his glass, shaking the ice around before downing it.

* * *

That day at Smitty's house had never really sat right with Dayvid, but it was eating at him even more now that he was confined to his cell under twenty-four hour, high security watch in a segregated unit. Dayvid was not housed with other prisoners, partly due to his case's high profile but mainly because of the power he held. Separating him, eliminated the potential coercion of other inmates

and prison staff. And after the recent escape of his sister, Fallon, prison officials weren't taken any chances.

The facility's solitary housing unit, or the "shoe" as it was referred to, was run by Sargent Roberts and his goon squad of officers, who led unprovoked attacks on inmates enforcing their brand of vigilante justice. Roberts, a bald and beefy, 23 year veteran with a vile temper, was hardest amongst the hard asses and the most brutal.

The unit had sixty identical 6 by 9 cells. Each had no windows or bars with concrete floors and cinder block walls. The cell doors were solid metal with narrow slots that served as entries and exits for food trays and were barely wide enough to allow prisoners to stick their wrists in and out to get handcuffed.

Roberts instructed the guards not to allow Dayvid to shower upon his arrival. It was a tool he used to break new inmates. After a few days he cracked his cell and turned on the fire hose dousing Dayvid, leaving him soaked and sore from being slammed against the wall by the strong steam of water. That was Dayvid's first encounter with Roberts, but it wouldn't be his last.

He was only to be let out of his cell to see his lawyer, or go to his preliminary hearings, which were to be held in Baltimore in two weeks. Being cut off and isolated from the world would drive a lesser man insane, but Dayvid passed the time exercising and piecing together the events that landed him in custody, mainly who was responsible for him being locked away.

The Porters had made plenty of enemies over the years, including Linx, who Dayvid had shot once upon a time. Linx got money but he was never about no gunplay and it was right up his alley to do some sucker shit like go to the feds in order to gain some get back. But even still, Fallon hadn't been in contact with the nigga in a minute, even though Dayvid knew she had continued seeing him for a while after she said she wasn't. There was no way possible he knew about the heist or the safe house. No matter how Dayvid sliced it, it all kept coming back to one person, their mentor Smitty and his faithful words "It's not good to switch up, when you gotta good thing going." For days Dayvid had been replaying every conversation he had with him throughout the years, over and over. This muthafucka had the most to lose by us getting out the game and going to Mexico, he thought to himself. "How long has he been playing us?" Dayvid pondered. "Probably since the beginning," he answered out loud. In his heart he always felt there had been something Smitty wasn't saying about the relationship between him and their father. He had never been able to question Nanny about it, she died a few years before Smitty revealed that tidbit of information, something else Dayvid found strange. "This nigga been a snake the whole time, since day one. On everything I love, I'ma put that old muthafucka under the dirt."

* * *

Dear Dayvid, my twin, my kindred and sharing spirit,

What can I say that you don't already know? What the Porters so carefully spent our entire lives avoiding, finally came to fruition…we got caught. The other was trusting outsiders. Because of that violation, the very rule the many warriors and gangsters before us, we now have to pay for it with our lives. That irreparable oversight came in form a mentor, father figure and confidant – Smitty, who put all of us in this position. Slow down, bro I can already feel the blood rising to your head and you want spazz the fuck out, but don't. You don't want to signal any emotions to them cracker guards who are probably no more than three feet away from you as you read this letter. Just follow Mr. Morganstein directions, he down for us. So, be cool for now and try to remember everything I tell you, because you cannot take this paper back with you.

Anyway, Smitty don't matter anymore, 'cause I handled that shit. If you know me, you'd know what I do to anyone that hurt my family. Plus, this nigga killed my girl Laura. I'm going to be straight up with you D; you are not getting out of prison alive. I hired the best money can buy, who worked on and built cases on niggas that ain't do a tenth of what we did. They have so much evidence on us, it'll take about ten seconds to send us away to prison for two hundred years, and I feel certain we can't live with that. As we speak, I am going mad just thinking about you sitting in there all alone and trapped. I feel we can't go through another day of these terrible times. But I do have some good news that will change everything…Fallon and Autumn are out of prison. They are on the run, but at least they are not locked up, and most of all they are safe. What I'm going to tell you next is our way out of this. Dayvid, we were born in a world where the only thing we knew was death, survival, drugs and crime. That's the hand that we were dealt. We were predisposed and predestined to that way of life. Right before Smitty met his maker, he said something to me that made me think. He said, "Nobody gets out of the game once you're in the thick of it, Rain. You knew that. If you in for a penny, you in for a pound, and ain't no in between. You married to this shit and the only way out for motherfuckers like us is death!" He was right, which is why we were really feeling that Mexico shit from the first thought. We were doing it for Fallon and Autumn's sake, as we should have from the very beginning. But you know it as well as me that our little sisters never were cut like us. Even though we all had the same mother and father, I always felt like they weren't built to be like us. Like me and you took all the stronger genes. Do you remember when Miss Jackie kept warning us, "You can change a cucumber into a pickle, but you can't turn a pickle back into a cucumber." I finally figured out what she meant by that recently. It means that when you're young you still have a chance of a life of crime getting a hold on you, but if you continue, it becomes you and knows no other life and you don't know when the cast hardened. There was no turning back for people like me, you, Nanny or even Smitty. Fallon and Autumn are still cucumbers, and I'm satisfied with that, and I can go peacefully with a clear conscience. Dayvid, I hope you understand where I'm going with this, and that's the reason I'm writing you this letter in the first place. We going to Jim Jones this shit and I'm not talking about the rapper. With that said, the next time you see my face, that's when it's going down. But we are taking a whole lot of people on vacation with us. If you agree to these terms, I want you to sign this paper with your signature, more so, as a front for the cameras that are watching you. Close the folder and tell Mr. Morganstein, "I understand my charges and accept the terms and conditions that you will represent me." Well, bro, it isn't too much left to say besides I love you to death and will see you soon.

P.S. Do not worry about Fallon and Autumn. I have them set up financially for years to come, because along with our money, Smitty gave up his stash of money and diamonds before he died. Well, kind of. I took his keys and the nigga wasn't as smart as we thought, 'cause he left his fortune stashed all throughout his house. (If you still don't trust that this is me....74261.)

Eternal peace, bro. I love you.

Your sister Rain.

Dayvid leaned back in his seat just a bit as he let his twin's proposal soak in. *Live Fast & Die Rich,* he thought to himself. That was what he and Rain used to tell one another. She was right, after everything they had done in life it was only fitting that they would go out in a blaze of glory. He was only fooling himself to think otherwise, niggas like him didn't retire and grow old on a beachfront property somewhere. They either died in a hail of bullets in the street or rotted away in prison. Dayvid had willingly assumed the risk that came with the life, fully accepting the possibility of dying in the streets but rotting away in the federal prison system wasn't an option. If he was gonna go out he preferred it be on his terms. As he lifted the pen off the table to sign his name, suddenly Nova's face was all he could see, vividly, almost like a hologram causing him to hesitate briefly. David thought for a second, flipped the paper over and scribbled something down.

"I need you to do me a favor, Mr. Morganstein." Dayvid said as he looked up from the papers, staring the man directly in his eyes expressing the seriousness of his statement. Then he signed his name on the paper and slid the pile back to the lawyer.

3

"When a lion or a bear came and carried off a sheep from the flock, I went after it, struck it and rescued the sheep from its mouth. When it turned on me, I seized it by its hair, struck it and killed it." *-1 Samuel 17:34-35*

Dayvid stood in the shower letting the water run over his head as if he was washing away his sins. At peace with the suicide mission he had signed up for, Dayvid's only concern was Nova. He knew the message he had sent through Mr. Morganstein would hit her like a sledgehammer shattering her world into even smaller fragments then it probably already was with him being behind bars. He wanted to spare her the emotional stress of having to watch him sit in a courtroom with his life hanging in the balance. He knew Nova would show up every single day and endure the torture of a trial, but that was a cross Dayvid preferred not to bear. She had been through too much already and no matter how much it pained him, he had to let her go. Her happiness meant more to him than her support. Dayvid was willing to do whatever to protect her, it had always been that way.

* * *

May 2002

The slamming of the front door shook the quiet row house waking Nova from her sleep. Looking over at the clock on the nightstand she struggled to make her sleepy eyes focus on the little red digits, finally they locked in and she could see that it was 1:27 in the morning. She knew it could only be one person and by the heavy thuds of footsteps and loud noises she could tell he was drunk again. Ronnie Simmons, or Redd as he was called by everyone, had been with Nova's mother since she was 11 years old. The former high school basketball star was a fixture in the neighborhood, it was well known that he sniffed heroin and drank a little too much. Two habits that seemed to increase after the recent drug overdose of Nova's mother. Despite his dependencies, Redd was able to hold down a steady job and people around the neighborhood commended him for continuing to take care of Nova after her mother's death. But Nova wasn't one of those singing his praises, she knew the ugly truth about him, she saw a side of him that nobody knew about. Redd had been molesting Nova since the age of 12. It all began as soon as her young body started to take shape, Nova's breasts were large for her age and her thick thighs and curvy hips had been inherited from her mother, arousing the predator inside of Redd. He wasted no time stripping the young girl of her innocence. Getting her mother high one night, then sneaking into Nova's room forcing himself on her after her mother had nodded off in one of her dope comas. The late night attacks continued with Redd using the threat of violence against her mother to keep her quiet. The sexual abuse had become more frequent after her mother's recent passing.

Nova's body froze with fear when she heard his footsteps stop in front of her door, she had hoped he was too drunk to be bothered with her tonight. She held her breath as Redd attempted to twist the door knob but it was locked. He tried a few more times before giving up and Nova felt the tension in her body disappear as she heard his front steps walk away from her door. Taking a deep breath, she allowed her body to relax as she turned over pulling the covers up and closing her eyes.

The sound of her door crashing in frightened her, causing her body to jerk in surprise as her heart skipped a beat in her chest. Redd stood in her doorway looking like a man possessed as he growled like a bear and his chest heaved up and down from the adrenaline pumping through him after breaking down the door. Nova threw the covers off of her and tried to leap from the bed to escape the room but Redd grabbed her by the neck tossing her back onto the bed. She tried screaming but before she could get out a sound, he had his huge hands over her mouth and all his weight on top of her 15-year-old body. He reeked of liquor. It was as if he had bathed in it. The loud smell made Nova sick to her stomach and her skin crawled as he laid on her, breathing in her face.

"Don't fight it, you lil bitch," Redd demanded through clenched teeth as his grip over her mouth tightened, muffling her screams even more. He tugged at her shorts aggressively until the sound of them ripping filled the room; he did the same to her panties exposing her bare bottom. "If you scream, I'll kill you, you little bitch. Do you understand me?"

Nova didn't reply. She just continued kicking her feet trying to wiggle free.

"You think I'm playin," Redd asked taking his forearm and putting most of his weight across her neck cutting off her air supply.

Nova tried her hardest to get air into her lungs but was unsuccessful. Feeling like her windpipe was being crushed she thought she was going to die. Nova began coughing uncontrollably as he finally released the pressure allowing her to take in air. No longer able to fight, Nova felt him pry her legs open bruising her thighs in the process. She felt the tip of his erect penis as he tried jamming himself into her a few times before finally succeeding. Nova felt a pain in her stomach as he rammed himself in and out of her grunting and groaning with every pump. Tears rolled down her face as she suffered in silence trying to take her mind to another place while he defiled her body. After a few minutes, she felt him pull out of her and ejaculate on her legs and stomach, spilling his seed on her bed as well.

Redd rose to his feet, sweat dripping from his brow and fixed his pants. "Get up and go clean yourself up," he instructed her before walking out of the room leaving a sore and crying Nova in his wake.

* * *

Nova bounced her leg up and down nervously as she watched the traffic go up and down her block. She had been waiting for weeks for this night to come. David had too, he loved spending time with Nova everything about her was perfect to him. From her around the way girl cool and her deep conversation to her thick curves and beautiful features. Tonight, she looked absolutely flawless to him, standing outside her house awaiting his arrival, wearing a yellow spaghetti strapped sundress. Her hair was pinned to one side letting her long flowing curls hang. She didn't need any make-up, her skin was blemish free, smooth and golden. Nova had a round beauty mark on the side of her right eye near her temple that enhanced her beautiful face. She wore her cherry lip gloss that accentuated her full lips and sported the diamond stud earrings Dayvid had bought her weeks before. For her sixteenth birthday, Dayvid had plans on taking her out for dinner at her favorite spot. He initially wanted to take her to one of those fancy spots he used to hear about but that really wasn't Nova's style, so she refused. It wasn't hard to tell by the expensive gifts and knots of money that Dayvid was doing okay for himself financially. Running the streets at night and doing robberies with his sisters was bringing in some nice cash. The Porters spent most of their nights sticking up drug houses and anybody who they knew had it for that matter. Dayvid didn't mind spending his paper on his girl either. Nova knew whatever Dayvid was doing was not safe or legal just by the large amounts of cash he would have on him, too much for any 16-year-old. However, she would never ask too many questions. They had a silent understanding. Nova knew her boyfriend was respected in the streets already at his age and she liked it. She felt safe with Dayvid and that was what mattered to her.

The two lovebirds decided to go to Sterling's, they had the best coddies and Nova wanted some for her birthday. Afterwards, the two had plans on getting a room at a nice hotel downtown. Tonight, was the night Dayvid hoped Nova would let him explore her body. He had remained patient when it came to sex with her. He knew she was a virgin and never wanted to pressure her into giving him her body before she was ready. Her mind was what always attracted him to her, she was smart and that was sexy to him. He wanted to create forever with her, so he would wait however long it took for the opportunity to touch her body. Tonight, was going to be special and the butterflies in Nova's stomach reminded her with every flutter.

"What up Slim, you look too good to be standing out here all by yourself," Dayvid flirted as he approached her.

Nova face lit up seeing her handsome beau approaching the steps. "Oh, I'm good. I'm waiting on this fine ass, light skin nigga to come get me, so I can spend all his money for my birthday," Nova playfully teased.

"Oh yeah, he sounds like a bamma. I'ma wait wit you so I can rob em when he shows up," he joked as he grabbed her off the steps and twirled her around. Dayvid already stood over with being six foot tall and slim, but solid and cut up at sixteen. Nova felt light as a feather in his arms. She loved her manchild and all his sexiness. Every time he would wrap her in his arms, she felt all was right in the world. "I got something to match that pretty dress you're wearing," he said putting her back down on her feet, reaching in his back pocket pulling out a rectangle shaped box. Nova smiled showing all of her pretty white teeth knowing it was a piece of jewelry in the box.

"You didn't have to Dayvid, you're always buying me something," she cooed as Dayvid opened the box and pulled out a diamond tennis bracelet.

"Be quiet and give me your wrist," he said.

Nova extended her arm on cue, so that he could clamp the bracelet on her wrist. "Oh my God," she said in amazement.

"I'm supposed to buy you nice things. That's what a real man does for his woman."

"I love it Dayvid!" Nova wrapped her arms around his neck and squeezed.

"And I love you."

Their young love was rare and true. Their hearts were like two magnets. It was as if they were born to be together, even at the age of sixteen they knew they wanted to be together forever.

* * *

"We don't have to do this if you don't want to," Dayvid whispered. "I'll wait however long it takes," he assured her.

Nova was lying on her back on the bed in the hotel as Dayvid kissed and licked all over her body. He stared up at her between placing wet kisses on her love flower. Her light moans seemed as though she was enjoying it but Dayvid could feel the tension in her body. Her legs weren't relaxed, and he knew her well enough to know she wasn't giving in to him freely.

"No, it's no pressure from you, there is just some things that I have not been all the way honest with you about," she spoke nervously as her voice began to crack.

Dayvid sat up, picked Nova up and sat her on his lap like he would always do. "Talk to me ma, what haven't you told me? You know you can tell me anything. We don't keep nothin' from each other," he said slightly confused. "What's up?"

"I know Dayvid, but I lied to you," she stood up in an attempt to put distance between them. She started to gather her clothes that were scattered on the floor on the hotel room. Tears welled in her eyes and began streaming down her cheeks.

"Lied to me about what?" Dayvid asked, anxious to hear what she was going to reveal. "Lied about what Nova?" he repeated.

"Dayvid, I'm not a virgin and I haven't been one for a long time," she blurted out.

Caught off guard by what she was saying, Dayvid tilted his head back and looked at her strangely. The girl whom he considered perfect had just told him something that took him for a loop. Something she could have been said and he wouldn't have thought any different of her. But the fact that she hadn't, had him thinking differently of her now.

"You lied to me about that, why? You could have just told me you gave another nigga some. I ain't tripping on that. What you thought I wouldn't fuck with you or I would love you less?" Dayvid asked staring her in the face. "I don't fuck with nobody outside of my sisters but you. You the only one who knows everything about me. Shit my sisters don't even know, so for you to lie to me," he paused letting his voice tail off. "Means more than you give some nigga some ass."

The tears continued to run down Nova's face as a pain grew in her stomach seeing the look of disappointment and frustration on Dayvid's face. She quickly grabbed her bag and headed towards the door.

"Where are you going Nova?" Dayvid jumped up from the bed and pulled her back by her arm, but she would not turn around to face him.

"You don't understand Dayvid," she spoke through tears continuing to stare at the door. "I didn't give it to anyone, it was taken from me," she cried out. "Almost every night since I was 12, he's been raping me," finally saying it out loud, she turned and collapsed into Dayvid's arms.

"What you telling me, ma? Who took it from you? Say his name." Although Dayvid knew who she was referring to, he needed to hear it.

"He would come in my room when my mom was passed out high. At first, I would cry and hold my breath, I couldn't stand his smell…I still can't," she said at the vivid memories. "He always reeked of alcohol when he came into my room for sex. I guess he has to get himself drunk to do it. Eventually it was just a routine."

"You never told your mother?"

"The one time I tried to tell my mother what he was doing to me, they argued all weekend until he beat her until her eyes were shut. She missed work for a whole week then blamed me for being a fast ass little girl and told me I had to get a job to make up the money she missed at work. That was what she said Dayvid, she blamed me," Nova cried out tears falling uncontrollably. "She told me I was a liar and I was disrespectful, and I didn't want her to be with no one. I wanted her to die by herself and I was trying to run her man off. She would tell me that she hated that I was born. That if she would've just aborted me like my real father asked, he would have never left. Then she told me, if I opened my mouth again, he would hurt her worse than the last time and it would all be my fault. So, I laid there and I didn't move; I counted the seconds in my head and wished he would hurry up and finish so that I could go to sleep."

Dayvid stood still and silent, digesting what Nova was telling him. The love of his life hurt night after night and he knew nothing about it. The rage he felt inside was like none he had felt before. His head felt like it was on fire as he thought of the things he planned to do to her predator. "Just say his name Nova," was all he could say.

"Redd," Nova managed to mumble off her lips. At that moment she couldn't manage to make eye contact with the only person she had shared her secret with.

"He's never going to touch you again, you hear me," Dayvid said lifting Nova's face so he could look in her eyes. "You don't ever have to lower your head in shame around me or nobody else. He'll never hurt you again, I'm going to make sure of it." He put both of his hands on her face and kissed her forehead. His voice was calm but stern and she felt safe hearing the words he spoke. Little did she know the monster that was forming inside of him craved the blood of the man who hurt her. He began to wipe the tears that were streaming down her face and held back ones of his own as Nova buried herself into his broad chest. He felt anger and grief because the person he loved the most in the world was being tormented but still she managed to hide her pain through smiles and laughter. Nova was the strongest person he had ever met. She was the only one who could make his heart smile, but inside she was broken. Someone had violated her, defiled her body and destroyed her mental to where she couldn't make love to the man she loved. All of this fueled his fire. "He's going to pay I promise. He took from you and now I'm gonna take from him."

Nova stopped and looked up at Dayvid. "What you going to do? I don't want anything to happen to you. I can't take anything happening to you." Nova began to fidget with the sleeves of his shirt, something she did often when she became nervous.

"Don't worry yourself, I'ma be good. I'm your man, right?"

"Yes," she quickly replied.

"Okay then know I got you and I got this," he kissed her cheek and flashed her that million dollar smile that would make any girl tingle. He wanted her to feel safe again and free from this nightmare she was forced to relive night after night. He wanted to be her safe haven, her place of peace. Nova returned the smile. The two never made love that night but just held each other as Dayvid stroked her hair until she fell asleep in his arms. He never shut his eyes; he remained awake and created a mental blueprint on how he was going to end Nova's pain.

* * *

Dayvid stood in a small alley between two homes directly across the street from Nova's house, tucked in the shadows on a rainy night with a black hoodie tied securely over his head. His heart was pounding in his chest like a bass drum from a marching band as he

gripped the rubber handle on the .38 special he had concealed inside his hoodie. Dayvid took a few deep breaths trying to calm his 16-year-old nerves. Only an adolescent, he had long lost his innocence to the Baltimore streets but had never taken a man's life. His nervousness slowly turned to anger as the horror stories Nova had shared replayed in his young mind. Strangely, his rage brought him a sense of calm and the pace of his rapidly beating heart began to slow down. His senses were heightened as time seemed to slow down and he felt as though he could hear every raindrop hitting the ground.

Dayvid's grip on the stainless revolver tightened when he spotted his target briskly walking up the block on the opposite side of the street. Dayvid stepped out of the alley and made his way across the street, walking with purpose towards the man heading his way. Clenching his jaw as he approached the man, he slowly began removing the pistol from his hoodie and let his arm rest at his side. Now right up on his unsuspecting victim, only a house away from Nova's, Dayvid leaned in with his shoulder and bumped the man as hard as he could, knocking him slightly off balance.

"Yo, watch where the fuck you're going, lil' nigga," the man shouted angrily at Dayvid as he turned to face him.

Dayvid turned, lifting his head to get a good look at the man. Staring directly in the man's face he had all the confirmation he needed. It was definitely Redd, Nova's stepfather. Without saying a word Dayvid lifted his gun so that it was even with the man's face and squeezed without any hesitation.

Dayvid's body went numb as he watched the man's head snap back from the impact of the bullet dropping him to the ground. Almost serene like, Dayvid stood over him placing the revolver in his mouth and pulling the trigger once again. The young killer stared in amazement as a cloud of smoke released from his victim's mouth. Dayvid ran down the block disappearing into the same shadows he had emerged from.

Nova hearing the sound of gunshots, peered out the window just in time to see a young man running down her block into the alley across from her house. His build and movement rang so familiar to her, causing a feeling of nervousness in the pit of her stomach. Nova glanced over at the digital clock on her nightstand and realized that this was the time her stepfather usually was on her block on his way home from work. She slipped on a pair of flip flops and raced downstairs and out into the street, joining the people who had slowly started spilling from their meager homes.

Reaching the crowd that was gathering just up the block from her house, Nova got a glimpse of the man on the ground. Her mouth dropped in shock and her heart sped up and she began feeling like she was going into cardiac arrest. Nova's stepfather laid with a pool of blood forming around his head and her mind immediately thought back to the young man she saw fleeing the scene. She was now sure it was Dayvid and she knew exactly why he had done what he had done. Nova lowered her head as tears raced down her face and neighbors rushed over to console her. They had no idea the monster her stepfather was and saw her tears as her showing grief; after all she had lost her mother only months prior. Only Nova knew they were tears of joy, she had finally been freed from the sexual predator that had consistently ravaged her young body. Her teenage love was now an unbreakable bond, Dayvid had sealed in blood. His secret was safe as Fort Knox with her just as hers had been with him.

Dayvid came to visit her two nights later to check on how she was doing and for the first time in Nova's life she gave her body to someone without being forced and it felt good.

* * *

Present Day

Nova placed the small box on her bed and sat down next to it. It had been a few weeks since Dayvid and his sibling's arrest and her nerves were shot. Her heart had almost jumped out her chest when she first heard the pounding on the door from the UPS delivery woman. No one outside of Dayvid knew where she resided so she definitely was surprised hearing the knock a few minutes ago. Nova hadn't been resting properly the past few weeks and it had started to show. She was jumpy and her skin looked dry and dark circles had formed around her doe eyes. She didn't look healthy at all and had dropped a pants' size due to her refusal to eat. Unable to get in contact with anyone who could provide her with any information about Dayvid was rapidly driving her crazy. He wouldn't want her to come to the jail and visit because that would surely put the feds on to her. But it had become harder and harder to fight the urge. Like the rest of the world she was glued to the news nightly trying to piece together as much information as she could. The Porter sisters' adventures while on the run had been the lead story on channels 2, 4, 6 & 7, but little was said about the man she loved. It was almost like he had disappeared in the system.

Opening the small box, she turned it over and a key fell out on to the bed along with a small piece of paper. Picking up the paper her heartbeat quickened when she recognized Dayvid's chicken scratch handwriting. Staring at the paper, Nova could make out what looked to be an address, which didn't ring familiar to her leaving her a little confused as to what Dayvid was trying to tell her. Holding the box in her hand, she could feel that it still had something in it, reaching inside she removed a CD. Seeing The Black Album, the classic CD by Jay-Z, Nova immediately knew what Dayvid was telling her. Upon release, the CD was billed as the legendary MC's last, he was supposed to back out of the game afterwards. To Dayvid and Nova the term "Black Album" held similar meaning, Nova knew Dayvid was telling her to back out, abort and go. She leaped off the bed racing into her closet in search of a bag that she could throw a few things in. Settling on a black leather Gucci duffle bag that belonged to Dayvid, she began filling it up as fast as she could. Re-entering the bedroom she tossed the bag onto the bed and walked over to her nightstand. Sliding open the drawer Nova snatched the .380 Dayvid had given her and stuffed it into the bag before zipping it up and throwing it over her shoulder. Nova was out the front door in no time. She had no problems leaving the apartment behind, it had been purchased under a fake name so there was no chance of it coming back to her or Dayvid if anyone was to come snooping around.

Pulling up to the curb and putting her car in park, Nova looked in her rearview mirror the same way she had the entire 30 minute ride. When she was sure she hadn't been followed she grabbed her pocketbook off the passenger seat, slipped her oversize shades on her face and exited the vehicle, crossing the street heading right into Maryland Savings & Loan.

Dayvid had a pair of fake IDs made for them a while back, showing them as a married couple. Something told her that this may have been the reason he was always thought three steps ahead. As the bank manager approached, Nova reached in her bag and removed the ID.

"Hello ma'am, how may I assist you today?" the woman asked.

"I need to get into my safe deposit box," Nova said calmly while flashing a smile at the woman.

"No problem, I'll just need your name and ID, as well as your key," the manager informed her.

"Renee Preston," Nova replied convincingly before removing her shades and handing over the ID and key.

"I'll just be one second Mrs. Preston," the woman said as she disappeared into her office.

Nova's heart was pounding in her chest and her nerves were all over the place. She felt as if she was being watched or followed and was beginning to wonder why the manager was taking so long to come back. *Maybe she knows it's a fake ID, this bitch is probably calling the cops,* Nova thought to herself. She glanced at the door of the bank contemplating if she should walk right out of it and not look back. The longer the woman was gone the faster her heartbeat. Finally, the manager emerged from her office sporting a smile on her face.

"Sorry I took so long. We just updated our systems and we've been having some issues," the woman explained. "Will Mr. Preston be joining you?"

"No not today," Nova answered wishing the lady would stop running her mouth and just let her get what she came for.

"Ok right this way Mrs. Preston."

Nova was quickly escorted to a private room filled with safe deposit boxes. The manager used the key to unlock the box and pulled a lock metal box out and placed it on the table in front of her before stepping out of the room. Once she was alone, Nova unlocked the latched box and took a peek at the contents inside. Her eyes got wide and round as marbles looking at the stacks of dead presidents staring back at her. A little over a million in cash, separated individually in ten thousand dollars stacks with mustard colored

currency bands on them. Nova picked up the note that laid on top of all the cash. It was from Dayvid and it read:

If you're reading this, chances are I'm dead or needing to be dead to you. I love you Nova and no matter what, I need you to always remember that. But we've come to a point that we both knew was a possibility in the life I choose and what I'm about to ask you to do is the hardest thing I've ever had to do. But I need you to let me go and move on with your life and never look back. The money in this box is enough for you to go anywhere you want and start anew. And for both of our sakes that's what I need you to do.

Love,

Your King.

Nova felt like she had been stabbed in the heart by a sword. The lump in her throat made it hard for her to swallow as tears rolled down her face faster than she could wipe them away. Not wanting to arise suspicion, Nova removed the cash from the box placing it into her oversized Birkin's bag and headed out the bank as fast as she had entered. Her mouth felt like cotton as she hurried to her vehicle fighting back more tears. Opening her door, she slipped in and put her bag on the passenger seat and frantically began searching for the keys. She was losing her mind and on the verge of a nervous breakdown. Her hands trembled as she finally located her keys but by then it was too late. The tears were flowing again and this time she gave into them, crying hysterically inside the privacy of her car. *Why is Dayvid sending me away like some child on punishment,* she thought to herself. *Doesn't he know how much I love him?* she wondered only wanting to be there for a man who had been there for her so many times throughout her life. Dayvid had his sisters, but they couldn't do for him what she did, and they rarely saw the side of him she had. He was her soul mate and she just couldn't forget about and move on. He needed her more than ever, but he was choosing to push her away. She wiped her face and searched her bag for her shades to hide her puffy red eyes. Slipping them on, she started the car and pulled off with no idea of where she planned on settling down and making a new life for herself, one that regretfully wouldn't include Dayvid.

4

"It makes no difference how good a man's case is. He will receive no audience with the king unless he can bribe his way into the king's presence." -*Absalom, son of David*

The clicking sound of David Banks' dark brown Bruno Magli shoes echoed the halls of the building as he strolled across the Supreme Court of the United States seal on the floor in route to his father's office. As the current Secretary of Homeland Security, he answered directly to the President of the United States and his primary duty was to protect the country and its citizens. Considered one of the most powerful men in the country, Banks oversee the U.S. Coast Guard, Border Patrol, Secret Service and FEMA. But his power didn't extend to the FBI, making his visit far more urgent than the usual. Banks needed his father's help getting his newfound son out of the clutches of federal custody. There was only one problem; the two men were barely on speaking terms, a fact he had conveniently failed to disclose to his daughter Rain.

Banks approached the door that read Chief Justice of the United States, The Honorable Harrison J. Banks and knocked a few times.

"Come in," said a husky voice from the other side of the door.

Entering the large corner office was like walking into the annals of history. Pictures of his father administering the oath of office to the last three presidents hung next to pictures of Judge Banks surrounded by other Supreme Court judges throughout the years. A quick survey of the photos on his desk told the story of a man with many powerful friends. Including the one of him and his golf buddy George H.W. Bush, who offered him the Director of the CIA position when he was in office, but he declined. Judge Banks enjoyed being the highest judicial officer in the country and the power that comes with it.

The sight of David immediately drew the ire of the judge. The elder Banks had never been one to mince his words and pulled no punches when it came to dealing with his son. The two men frequently bumped heads throughout David's life on everything; from the type of people he hung around, the music he liked to the choice of his career. There was always friction between the two strong personalities, something Mrs. Banks had always been able to smooth over and manage. But a stalemate had ensued between the two after her death a year ago.

"Well, well, look what the cat dragged in," Judge Banks snidely remarked upon seeing his son, his displeasure clearly on display. "Did you ride over here on your high horse?"

"Hello dad," David replied ignoring the old man's remarks. "How you been?"

"Cut the shit David," the judge said preferring to skip the insincere pleasantries. "What do you want? Because I know you want something, you always want something."

David sat in the chair in front of his father's desk and got right to it. "You remember a friend of mine? A girl by the name of Remy?" he asked, feeling his body temperature increase from the anger he felt for what his father had done.

"Can't say that I do, not off hand," he replied.

David knew his father was lying, the elder Banks had a memory like an elephant. He remembered the names and charges of every defendant that had ever graced the wall of his courtroom. So, David found his sudden case of amnesia hard to believe. "Looks like you're the one who needs to cut the shit," he stated sternly.

"Yeah I remember her. The little black girl that had your nose wide open after you got a taste of some sweet black pussy," the judge laughed. "Guess it's not true what they say huh? Once you go black you never go back."

David's menacing eyes burned a hole through his father as he gave him the death stare, unamused by the judge's sense of humor.

"Let me guess, your here about those God forsaken twins of yours," he bluntly announced.

David couldn't believe his ears, not only had his father run off the love of his life, but he had known about the existence of his children and had hid it from him all these years. Everything in him wanted to put a bullet through his father's head as he sat there with a smug look on his face.

"What you thought I didn't know?" the judge asked. "I've been in this town a lot longer than you son. I know where all the bodies are buried, there's no secret I don't know or haven't heard," he assured his son. "You are not the only powerful man in this family."

"You knew, all this time you knew. Why would you keep something like that from me? You're an evil old bastard, you always were. I don't know how mom put up with you all those years."

"Don't get me started on your mother. She had a soft spot for those blacks just like you and believe me she was no saint either," he spat. "Of course I knew, you should thank me. I been saving you from yourself for years. Blacks and whites do not and should not mix. There was no way in hell you would have been able to reach the pinnacle of this profession with that black girl on your arm. Now what do you want?" Judge Banks said beginning to grow frustrated with the back and forth.

"These kids need our help. They are in way over their heads and I feel we owe it to them to do whatever we can to get them out of trouble and out of dodge," David expressed.

"I don't owe those lowlife mutts a thing and you don't either. You should be running in the opposite way from them. If the word gets out that these menaces to society are in any way connected to us, it can ruin everything I've worked my whole life to build. Have you seen the things they are accused of? They are rotten to the core and there is no help for them. I refuse to allow you or them to sullen the Banks family name."

"Sullen? You and I have done far worse in the name of government. Our hands are dirtier than most, or have you forgotten 9/11," he said looking down at the picture of the judge and the elder Bush. "Listen, I've already made Rain disappear but helping Dayvid is a little more difficult. He is locked in North Branch and I have no pull with the feds. So, I need your help."

"That was your doing? That whole explosion on the news thing?" Judge Banks shook his head in disbelief. "You always were a little over the top."

"Yes," David nodded. "Now I need your help."

Judge Banks leaned forward in his chair, resting his folded arms of his desk. "I can't even remember the last time I saw you. Oh yeah, your mother's funeral and now you show up in my office asking for a favor. One that could put both our careers in jeopardy," he barked. "I'm not helping you, matter of fact, I'm going to see to it myself that bastard son of yours gets a needle in his arm. And those two younger sisters of his too. So, if you want to do anything to help him, you tell him, he better take a plea and serve out the rest of his miserable days in that super max in Maryland. Cause if he goes to trial, he's a dead man."

David rose to his feet buttoning his suit jacket. The meeting with his father hadn't gone at all like he had hoped. "Good to know some things never change," he declared. "Nice seeing you again," he said sarcastically.

"Wish I could say the same," answered the judge.

* * *

"Back to the door Porter!" yelled Sgt. Roberts.

Dayvid heard the officer's voice bellow through the door as the small slot in his door slid open. Rising to his feet he turned his back to the door and slid his hands through the slot allowing for the officer to handcuff his wrists.

"Back away from the door and remain with your back to me," Roberts instructed.

The large metal door cracked open allowing light to enter the cell, blinding Dayvid. He had been locked in his cell for almost a week without being let out for his required one hour a day. The officers on duty pick and choose who they felt they wanted to let out, flexing their muscle showing the inmates who was in charge. They also would skip his cell when doling out food trays as well. Dayvid was locked in concrete hell. But he still wouldn't allow it to break him. He was mentally tougher than most and took everything in stride. His indifferent attitude got under Roberts skin and he would attempt to provoke Dayvid every chance he got.

"Turn around you piece of shit," Roberts demanded. "You know I heard they call this fucker the King," he said to the other officers who were placing shackles on Dayvid. The men all laughed in unison. "How those restraints feel, King? Are they good enough for you?" Roberts poked. "What'll you say we give Porter here a king's welcome?"

The guards began striking Dayvid's legs with their metal batons causing him to collapse to the floor in pain. Roberts watched in enjoyment as his goons pounded away at Dayvid as he laid on the ground writhing in pain. "Rodney King," quipped the sergeant. "OK, Ok, that's enough. Pick em up," he commanded after a few minutes.

"Arrgh," Dayvid groaned being yanked from the ground by his shackles.

Roberts got right into his face, the smell of coffee permeating on his breath. "There's only one King on this unit and that's me. Are we clear?" He didn't wait for Dayvid to answer instructing the guards holding him to take him away. "Get him outta my sight."

The officers led a shackled and battered Dayvid down a long corridor that led to an empty room with a table and a few chairs in it. The officers forcefully sat him down in one of the chairs and left the room, leaving him alone. Although he was in pain, Dayvid's demeanor and face remained unchanging as he sat calmly in the quiet room. The only sound being the chains he was in clanging together as he moved in his seat trying to find a comfortable position for his legs. After a few minutes the door of the room opened and a black female in her earlier forties, dressed in a dark blue pants suit with her hair pulled back into a tight bun, stepped in followed by a white man in an equally understated suit.

U.S. Marshals Veronica Torrence and Angelo Palmeri were part of the Government's fugitive task force and had been on the Porter sisters trail for almost a month, crisscrossing the country hoping to slap the cuffs on the trio. U.S Marshal Torrence had become obsessed with the Porter family and was suffering from an acute case of sleep deprivation trying to capture the fugitives. The smirk on her face showed that she was enjoyed seeing Dayvid shackled the same way she hoped to see his siblings. Palmeri took a seat while she paced around the room like a car on a NASCAR track.

"How are you doing today Dayvid? I'm U.S. Marshal Angelo Palmeri and this is my partner Veronica Torrence. We're a part of the fugitive task force and we've been assigned to your sisters' cases. I know you may not be aware, but those ladies have been causing quite a stir out in the world leaving dead bodies and a shot state trooper in their wake. Your sister Fallon slipped through our grasp and made it across the border into Mexico, but it won't be long before she slips up and we get another shot at her."

Dayvid just listened never showing any emotion but inside he was happy to hear Fallon made it to Mexico.

"Autumn won't be as lucky. Not only are we after her but she has one of the most ruthless drug kingpins hot on her trail. She would be best served turning herself in," she informed.

"What's with all the fucking updates," Torrence jumped in.

Dayvid had been watching her circle the room, it was obvious to him that this case was kicking her ass. Her face looked sunken in and she had dark, puffy bags under her eyes. Dayvid took a sense of pride in the fact that his sisters were out there giving them hell. Little did they know they hadn't seen nothing yet.

"Listen I came all this way to look you in your face and tell you that you are going to die in the federal prison system. Whether you rot away in here or they stick a needle in your fucking arm, you sorry son of a bitch. You will never breathe another breath of free air. You're gonna die in this godforsaken place, King Dayvid," Torrence took pleasure in taunting him.

Dayvid didn't give her the satisfaction of a reaction, never one to show his cards he remained stoic. Torrence had done her research and didn't expect him to react but she knew the folder in her hand would move the needle some with him.

"We are aware of you and Rain's little master plan Dayvid," Torrence informed him.

He immediately cursed Rain for trusting that fucking lawyer but he was about to learn he wasn't the culprit.

"Yeah, we know. But there is no chance in hell of that ever happening since your sister Rain is dead," Torrence announced, almost as if she was bragging as she slammed the folder down on the table in front of him.

Believing it to be another tactic of the government, Dayvid took what she said with a grain of salt.

"Oh, you don't believe me, huh? I thought you would know. Don't they say twins can feel each other," she mocked looking over at her partner.

"Rain attempted to buy explosives on the black market in hopes of breaking you out. But the feds received a tip and converged on the van. Rain fled and after a brief chase the van exploded in a field," Palmeri explained to Dayvid.

"Yeah, looks like she went through with her planned suicide without you," Torrence said flipping open the folder allowing him to see the pictures of the scene and newspaper clippings.

It was then that Dayvid knew it was true. He felt a pain he hadn't felt since standing in the cemetery watching his parents being lowered into the ground. Losing Rain was like losing a piece of himself. Fueled by rage Dayvid tried to leap from his chair and lunge at the Marshals but he was easily subdued due to his shackles and the pain shooting up and down his legs.

"Fuck you bitch," Dayvid screamed at U.S. Marshal Torrence. "I'ma put a bullet in your head and I'm gonna kill everybody you love, that's on my sister's grave," Dayvid promised the startled Marshal as officers rushed the room and began levying blow after blow on him before picking him up, leading him down the hall and tossing him back in his cell.

* * *

The sound of his cell opening made Dayvid sit up on his bunk. Although he didn't know the time, his body told him it was the middle of the night. Sergeant Roberts looked like the devil standing in the doorway holding a pump shotgun in his hand, with four of his minions behind him dressed in riot gear holding body shields in front of them.

"On your feet Porter," Roberts demanded cocking the gun and pointing it at him.

This muthafucka, Dayvid thought to himself as he slowly rose to his feet, unsure of what was the unpredictable men were up to. The evil grin on the faces of the officer alarmed him as he braced himself to deal with whatever was about to happen. Dayvid balled his fist up and put his back up against the wall ready to fight.

"Ha Ha Ha Ha," the sinister laugh of Roberts was sickening to his ear. "Save your energy, you're gonna need it. Now you can come on your feet or we can carry you, it's really up to you," he informed Dayvid aiming the shotgun directly at his head.

Dayvid lowered his guard as the officers stepped inside his cell and handcuffed him. He was forced to walk down a hallway to a service elevator as the officers walked closely behind him and Roberts kept the shotgun pointed at him. As the elevator doors opened, Roberts nudged the gun in his back making him step off. The large gathering of officers, in what looked to be the boiler room deep in the bowels of the jail immediately, caught his attention. The mass of men opened up and Roberts ordered for him to keep moving. Dayvid felt wads of spit hitting him as he made his way through the group of heckling officers. The rabid men formed a circle around him as one of the guards released his cuffs.

Dayvid looked around, still unsure of what was happening, until he saw the circle open up on the other side. Stepping into view was a hulking 6 foot 6, outlaw biker with long hair, a beard, and tattoos covering most of his body. Not a small man in his own right, the brawny monster dwarfed Dayvid.

"Here are the rules for the new guy," Roberts shouted over the crowd's ruckus. "You fight or you die, and you fight until one of you is dead!" he continued. "Now place your bets."

The room began shouting out the name of the competitor they were taking in the fight. "Norton," the name of the tatted up giant was an overwhelming favor in the room. But there were a few officers willing to bet on Dayvid.

Suddenly, the room grew silent and the circle got bigger just as a lead pipe and 3 pound sledgehammer was tossed in the middle of the two inmates. The crowd erupted as the two men raced to grab a weapon. Dayvid reached for the lead pipe, which was closer to him, but was rocked by a punch from Norton knocking him off balance and to the ground. Norton scooped up both weapons and tried to decide which one he would use as Dayvid laid on the ground trying to shake the cobwebs out his head. Norton tossed the lead pipe into the crowd, far out of Dayvid's reach, then came down with a powerful swing with the sledgehammer like Thor. Dayvid barely escaped the crushing blow as he rolled out the way and to his feet. The two men began circling one another, each man sizing up the other. Norton rushed Dayvid swinging his weapon wildly but missing with every attempt. Easily avoiding his opponent, Dayvid landed a combination of punches that landed flush, but one stunned him briefly. Norton thrust the sledgehammer into Dayvid's ribs a few times, stopping him from throwing anymore blows. He then landed a knee to his jaw followed by a blow to the back with the weapon, dropping Dayvid to the ground flat on his stomach and spitting blood from his mouth. Norton kicked Dayvid in the face opening a cut over his eye. Norton played to the crowd of officers as they called for him to end the fight. He dropped the sledgehammer to the ground and pulled a shank from under his shirt as they all went crazy.

Dayvid vision was becoming blurry from the blood dripping into his eye, but he could still see the Grizzly Adams looking biker approaching with the sharp object in his hand. Dayvid flipped the razor he held concealed in his mouth and spit it into his hand.

Norton grabbed a hand full of Dayvid's curly mane and attempted to lift him up to cut his throat. Dayvid swiftly came across the back of the biker's foot with the razor cutting his Achilles tendon in the process. Norton squealed like a stick pig, as he dropped his weapon and fell to the ground with blood pouring out the back of his foot.

A bloody Dayvid rolled over onto his wounded opponent pinning his arms down with his knees and began pounding Norton's face into a bloody pulp. The sound of crunching bone could be heard with every blow landed. Dayvid grabbed the shank from off the floor next to him as the crowd's boos grew louder. Dayvid repeatedly drove the shank into the side of Norton neck as blood squirted everywhere, not stopping until he was sure the man was dead.

Dayvid was covered in blood as he rose to his feet. Some of the blood was his, but it was mostly the man who lay dead at his feet. He scanned the crowd until his eyes landed on Sergeant Roberts, who by the look on his face was not happy with the outcome. Dayvid smirked.

"Gas him!" Roberts commanded.

The officers dressed in riot gear quickly approached Dayvid and sprayed him with pepper spray. He dropped to his knees trying to catch his breath, unable to breathe he began coughing violently until he was vomiting and spitting up blood.

"Take his ass to the infirmary," Roberts shouted, the evil grin returning to his face. Dayvid would learn one way or the other that he always got the last laugh.

* * *

A Week Later

Dayvid laid awake in the dark cell consumed with thoughts of his twin sister. Every time he closed his eyes, he saw her face and could hear her voice in his head so vividly he began answering it back. All through the night he jumped out of his sleep thinking he heard her in his cell. He was truly at his wits end and his sanity had begun to slip away. The news brought by the U.S. Marshals had done what North Branch and Sergeant Roberts had failed to do these past few weeks; break him mentally and spiritually. Dayvid contemplated suicide as he lay in his cell. He thought about trying to grab one of the officer's gun and having them shoot him to death, anything to ease the pain he felt. All these things ran through his mind as the darkness of the cell had begun to seep into him and eat at his once unbreakable will. Suicide was the easy way out though, something Dayvid frowned upon because it was for cowards, which was something he could never be. He began to reserve himself to the fact that he could possibly spend the rest of his days in a cell just like the one he was in. He felt his eyes becoming heavy and decided to try again to get some sleep.

He had finally fell into a deep sleep when he was awakened by the sound of his cell door being opened. A little groggy, Dayvid attempted to get to his feet. He hadn't heard an officer call his name or the slot slide open before his door was cracked. He was fully prepared for Roberts' goon squad reaching under his bunk for the shank he kept there. Just as he made it to his feet, he was rushed by some figures that he couldn't quite make out in the darkness of his cell. The shank fell to the ground forcing Dayvid to knuckle up and swing trying to connect on the first person he felt close to him. He was successful and heard a loud moan followed by a thud of a body hitting the floor after he connected flush on the person's jaw. Dayvid suddenly felt a shock of electricity shoot through his body and saw the flickering light of a taser illuminate his cell. No longer able to control his body, Dayvid's legs gave out and he came crashing to the floor before blacking out.

Slowly coming to, he could feel himself bouncing up and down and immediately knew he was riding in a vehicle that was moving at a pretty good speed. Opening his eyes, the darkness didn't give away to light like he expected. He quickly realized he had a cloth bag over his head. Dayvid's body ached and his head was banging, a result of hitting his head after being tasered.

After a while he felt the vehicle come to a stop and from the sound of the doors behind him opening, he knew he was in a van. Dayvid felt two sets of hands grab him and pull him from the van, then drag him across the floor before tossing him roughly into a chair. He was powerless to do anything due to his hands being tied behind his back. Dayvid heard the men that had dragged him to the chair go silent all of a sudden and he could hear the sound of shoes in the distance grow louder as they walked towards him then stop.

"Remove his hood," he heard the man's voice say and in a matter of seconds Dayvid could see everything that was in front of him. Looking around at his surroundings, he realized that he was in the middle of a dimly lit abandon warehouse. He counted four men

in suits, including the man standing directly in front of him. Dayvid and his sisters had robbed many men and made many enemies over the years and there was no telling who these guys were and what they had against Dayvid. The men looked like a professional hit squad for a major player. *Who else could pull strings to have me kidnapped out of federal custody,* he thought to himself. Dayvid had now seen it all and after going through so much he was ready to die. He sat up straight in the chair, spit on the floor and awaited to hear his fate.

"Hello Dayvid," the man standing in the shadows in front of him spoke.

Dayvid squint his eyes trying to make out his face but could only see his silhouette.

"I know you're a little confused as to what you're doing here. And I plan on explaining all that to you. I also plan on offering you a deal, a way out of all this trouble you're in. But first I need you to listen carefully to everything I say," the man said.

"You can stop right there slim. I ain't never told shit and I ain't about to start now, so you can keep your deal. And I would appreciate if you took me back to the jail and let me do my muthafuckin' time," Dayvid informed the mystery man.

"This deal won't require you to do any of that. Like I said, I need you to listen carefully," the man said finally stepping out of the shadows, allowing Dayvid to see him. "I'm David Banks, U.S Secretary of Homeland Security and I was friends with your mother,

Remy."

Dayvid tilted his head in disbelief looking at the white man in the suit standing in front of him. He had never remembered his mother having any white friends. He didn't even know she knew any white people for that matter. "How you know my mother?" he asked.

"I met your mother about a year before you and your sister Rain was born. Out of respect for her, I'm here to offer you a way out of all of this. A fresh start, a new beginning, a whole new identity. The same deal I gave your sister Rain."

"Fuck you mean the same deal you gave Rain," Dayvid fumed. "We're Porters. We don't make deals with people like you."

"Like you, Rain was reluctant at first but after hearing what I had to say she became receptive and agreed to the deal," Banks said calmly.

"Some fucking deal, Rain is dead. Who you think you fooling with this bullshit story? You gotta come better than that," Dayvid declared.

"Rain Porter is dead, but your sister is as alive as she's ever been," Banks informed him. "I have the power to make a lot of things happen. That thing with the van blowing up, that was me. Rain Porter is no more, she has a whole new identity and there's not a fed in the country after her."

The whole thing sounded a little too good to Dayvid, but he played along. "What about Fallon and Autumn?" he asked.

"My agency hasn't been able to locate them yet, but I have people on it, and they will receive the same deal."

"So, what I got to do? You want me to kill some politician or something," Dayvid inquired causing Banks to laugh.

"No none of that. All I ask is that you leave this life alone and disappear never to be heard from again," he explained.

"That's it?"

"That's it," the man responded.

"Let me ask you a question why you doing all this? How you say you know my mother again?"

David Banks lowered his head, breaking eye contact with Dayvid. "Your mother was a very special woman and she really meant a lot to me. She was a beautiful woman as well. I met her at a concert when I was in college and we dated for a brief time. Until my father came between us many, many years ago. Two weeks ago I received a visit from your mother's friend, Miss Jackie. And she shared with me a secret that your mother had only shared with her."

"And what was that," an anxious Dayvid quizzed.

"That I'm your father."

"Get the fuck out of here," Dayvid laughed. "My father's name is James Porter," Dayvid said. But inside it was always something he had wondered about because he and Rain were lighter than both their parents and their sisters. The white man standing in front of him would explain his light skin.

"It's true, I performed a DNA test on Rain. I'm you two's father.

My nickname for your mother was Raindrop and my name is David. That explains where you two got your names from," he explained.

Dayvid had always wonder why his mother hadn't made him a junior, naming him after the man he thought was his father, but it all made sense now. "I hope you're not expecting some kumbaya type moment," Dayvid said to his new ound father seeming indifferent about it all rather than shocked or angered. "I'm a little too old for the father-son baseball games and that ain't really my thing anyway."

Banks motioned for one of the men to release his son from his restraints while another man handed him a change of clothes. "Listen all I need is for you to lay low for 24 hours while I get all your new identification straight and come up with a story for the news to explain how you just disappeared from North Branch. Then off to Mexico you go."

"That's cool but I ain't going nowhere without Autumn. I know Fallon is already in Mexico but Autumn's not and I ain't going nowhere until I know she is safe. I heard she may be in some trouble. I gotta get my baby sister."

"Dayvid you have to trust me. I will get Autumn safely to Mexico, but I need you to disappear immediately. I'm putting my career on the line doing this," Banks stated. "None of this works if you go off the rail. I'm not gonna let anything happen to her."

Dayvid took a deep breath and thought a moment before reluctantly agreeing. "Ok but there is something I need to do before

I leave," Dayvid announced.

"What?"

"I have to get my girl, Nova, she's coming with me."

"Not happening," Banks told his son. "That's not part of the deal, you can no longer contact anyone who knew you as Dayvid Porter. That person is dead. That will put everything at risk. That can't and will not happen. This deal only pertains to you and your siblings, that's it."

"She won't say anything I'm willing to bet my life on it," Dayvid said.

"But I'm not," his father said frankly. "And I won't."

"Then you can take ya deal and shove it in your ass, sideways. Cuz, I ain't going nowhere without Nova." Dayvid said flaring his nose like he did when he became angry. Nova meant as much to him as any of his sisters and he was willing to spare her the pain and suffering of dealing with a lengthy drawn out court case. With a second chance he planned on doing all the things he and Nova had discussed when thinking about their future.

"Don't blow this Dayvid. If you walk out that door, all bets are off; you're on your own. There's nothing I can do for you," Banks pleaded with his son.

"I been on my own my whole life, that ain't nothing new. I never even knew you existed before now. I ain't need you then and Ion't need you now. I'm good in these streets," Dayvid brashly stated.

"If you get caught this meeting never happened," Banks said

realizing Dayvid's mind was made up.

"What meeting?" Dayvid said showing his father he fully understood what he was walking away from.

"Dayvid," Banks called out stopping him in his tracks as he walked towards the door. "At least lay low for a few hours, let me feed the news a story," then he nodded to one of the men, who slid his gun across the warehouse floor to Dayvid. "Good luck."

5

"Thou has shed blood abundantly and has made great wars: thou shalt not build a house unto my name, because thou has shed much blood upon the earth in my sight." *-1 Chronicles 22:8*

The rain had started to pick up its pace providing Dayvid with the perfect cover as he turned down Harlem Avenue in the Edmonson Village section of Baltimore. All the while keeping his hand close to the gun on his waist. Cutting through a path camouflaged by trees, he hopped a fence into the backyard of an attached brick two level home. Using his foot, Dayvid removed a pile of leaves off a slab of concrete before lifting it and grabbing the key he kept hidden underneath. The obscure basement apartment in the low-income neighborhood was onc place Dayvid knew he could go undetected.

He used the hideout only once before and knew no one would think to look for him there. Entering the dark apartment, his nostrils were greeted by the smell of stale air as he felt along the wall until he found the light switch and clicked it on. The light flickered a few times before fully coming on and lighting up the entire space. The small studio apartment consisted of a kitchenette, with raggedy white cabinets and a small refrigerator, a sleeping area with a pullout couch and a TV and a cramped bathroom with a standup shower. Dayvid began to remove his wet clothes, stripping all the way down to his boxer briefs before heading over to the closet. Hanging in the empty closet was an all-black hooded sweat suit along with a pair of never worn black timberland boots. Dayvid quickly grabbed the change of clothes and put them on. Since being in jail, he had shed a couple pounds making the clothes fit him a little loose than he expected but they would have to do for now. He clicked on the TV then headed straight to the bathroom to take a piss.

Staring in the mirror as he washed his hands, Dayvid barely recognized himself. His face was slimmer and his normally well groomed appearance had been replaced by a scruffy looking beard and a small curly afro. North Branch had really taken a toll on him, but he was back in his element so Dayvid could care less. His only concern was to get in contact with Morganstein to get the money Rain had left him with, find Nova then get to Mexico. Exiting the bathroom and entering the kitchenette area, Dayvid began searching through the drawers until he found a car key that belonged to a hoopty he kept stashed a block or so away. Opening the refrigerator, which he kept unplugged, Dayvid removed a brown paper bag from inside that contained a gun and ten thousand dollars in cash. He was anxious to hit the streets and make moves, but he knew he needed to lay low until his father could work his magic. He wasn't comfortable having to trust someone he didn't know but Banks had helped Rain and gotten him out of jail, so he was willing to give him the benefit of the doubt. He strolled back over to the pullout couch, plopping down on it and placing the bag next to him. With no other choice but to wait, Dayvid leaned his head back closing his eyes and let the sound of the TV help him drift off to sleep.

* * *

Nova had been lying in the bed for almost a week straight now. After driving around for what seemed like an eternity. She checked into The DuPont Circle Hotel in D.C and rented the grand deluxe room. This will be home for her until she decided on her next move. Nova closed herself out to the world and contemplated on what she would do with her life. She played around with the thought of leaving the Maryland-D.C. area for good, it really sounded like the best option for her with everything that was going on. She had a little over two hundred grand Dayvid had left her stashed in the hotel room safe and she couldn't decide what she wanted to do. Atlanta always sounded nice to Nova, she could easily relocate there and open her own business. She always had a love for doing hair and would practice on her own head until Dayvid started buying her mannequin heads so that she could practice on them. He offered to pay for her to go to cosmetology school so she could get her license, although she toyed with the idea many times, she never took it seriously. But now she was, after all what else would she do. "What would she do?" the million dollar question that was burning in her brain. It seemed so simple, but it wasn't. All Nova had ever known was Baltimore and Dayvid, but the love of her life was gone. He was her partner, her best friend, the only person in the world who was ever truly happy for her and genuinely loved her. And she was struggling with her emotions at just the mere thought of him no longer being in her life. He would surely be sentenced to rot away in a federal prison for the rest of his life or even worse, death. The Porter siblings had done so much, half of which she didn't care to imagine. Nova never saw the person the streets called King Dayvid. When she looked at him, she only saw Dayvid Porter, a man who would do anything to provide for and protect those that he loved. Dayvid's heart was as big as his reputation but it was his reputation and his actions that made him a list of enemies. Enemies who would not miss out on the opportunity to do something to him if the chance presented itself. He was feared yes, but he was hated more.

Nova reluctantly pulled the covers away from her face in effort to will herself to get up and shower. She scanned the room and noticed the mess she had accumulated over the past few days. There was days of room service piled on the floor and on the table that sat next to the plasma TV. She got up out the bed preparing to head into the bathroom to shower before doing so she grabbed the remote off the nightstand to turn the TV on. Nova walked in the bathroom and turned on the shower. Before stepping, she took a long look at her reflection in the mirror, noticing her swollen and puffy eyelids she wore from days of crying nonstop. She didn't look like her normal self or even felt like it. Nova pulled her messy hair back into a sloppy ponytail and was taken aback by the musky smell of her under arms.

"Damn I might need an extra five minutes in that bad boy," she spoke out loud to herself acknowledging the much needed shower she was about to take. Nova hadn't cared about much for the past week including her hygiene. She ordered room service just to pick through the food, only eating enough to coat her stomach as she blew through the fully stocked bar in the living room. Alcohol seemed to console her and ease her pain just enough to let her sleep through the majority of it. Nova wept for Dayvid because she missed him, but her tears were mostly out of anger. "How could he just cut me off like that?" she asked herself over and over again. "What made him think I could just move on with my life like everything was normal? Like we didn't have a life together, what about all our plans?" she asked while she cried. "Did he think I wasn't a strong enough woman to stand by him when the chips were down? I would do any bid no matter how long for that man. How could he not know?"

Nova tried to cope with her pain and anger towards Dayvid, she cried while letting the hot water hit her body and run down over her head. She wiped her face with the washcloth and briefly stepped out of the shower to reach for the shampoo by the sink when the television caught her attention. Through the door she saw Dayvid's mug shot in the top right corner of the screen. Nova rushed out the bathroom to turn up the volume so she could hear what was being said. Butterflies filled up her stomach giving her a feeling like she needed to use the bathroom and she started fidgeting from her nervousness. She pressed the volume button on the remote as fast as she could, not wanting to miss one word the reporter was saying, only to receive the worst news of her life.

"Good Evening, I'm MaryAnn Reynolds reporting live in front of the North Branch Correctional Institution. It what can only be described as an unforeseen turn of events, it's being reported that at 5 o'clock this morning the Notorious Dayvid Porter also known as "King Dayvid" was found dead in his cell. The cause of death is being called an apparent suicide. While prison officials have yet to release a statement, our sources on the inside are telling us that a guard found Porter's body slumped up against the door of his cell with his shirt around his neck," the reporter stated. "Hold on, we have just received confirmation that it is in fact true, Dayvid Porter is dead from an apparent suicide. We were just informed an official statement will be made shortly by the prison's warden. We will have that for you live in just a few minutes. Back to you guys in the studio."

Nova could not believe her ears or what she was seeing. The news hit her like a ton of bricks to her stomach. She immediately became light headed and dizzy as she let her naked body drop to the floor.

"Oh my God! Oh God, Nooooooo!" she screamed. "What the fuck are they talking about? Oh my God! Dayvid, what did you do?" she wondered aloud. "They're lying, they are fucking lying!" Nova spoke to herself trying to convince her mind and heart that what she just heard wasn't true. The pain she felt was though; it was one she never experienced before in her life. Not even when her mother overdosed or when her stepfather was killing her young mind and body every time he penetrated her. She felt broken, dead inside and betrayed by love. Dayvid was dead and now she truly was in the world by all by herself. Nova let out a scream, but no sound escaped her mouth, sort of like a baby gasping for air in midst of a cry. All that came out of her was the silent sound of pain. Nova wrapped her arms around her knees and laid her head on top of them as she rocked herself back and forth in agony. She wanted to die just so she could be with him again. At that moment nothing was worth living for and nothing mattered. Not how long she planned on staying in hotel, where she would go or how she planned to live the rest of her life. It all seemed meaningless without Dayvid. All she could do was drown herself in her tears. Nova mourned him and hated him at the same time. Life as she knew it had been forever changed. The look in her eyes was empty as if someone had turned off the light in her soul.

* * *

Dayvid adjusted the driver seat on the beat up '92 Acura Integra so that he could remain unseen while he kept an eye on the elevator of the underground parking garage. He had been lying in wait for almost two hours, waiting for Mr. Morganstein to emerge from the elevator in route to his car. Walking into his office wasn't an option for a man who was supposed to be dead but Dayvid needed the bread Rain had left with the lawyer and he needed it badly. The thing about being a bank robber and hit man is that you need to keep working to keep the money flowing and though the Porters had been able to make a good living for themselves, they didn't have a big stash. All the money from the Brinks heist had been seized and Dayvid needed to piece together what he could in order to get to Mexico.

The elevator door opened, and Mr. Morganstein stepped off into the parking garage and made a bee line to his Mercedes. Hitting the button on his remote starter, the luxury vehicle cranked up and unlocked as he marched towards it. Opening the back door, he tossed his briefcase in the back then slammed the door shut. Reaching for the driver's door he felt the cold steel of a Ruger 9mm pressed against the back of his neck.

"Get in the car, slowly," Dayvid demanded.

"Please, you don't have to do this," the petrified lawyer begged feeling his legs go stiff and his heart almost jump out his chest. He had always feared being car jacked and now it was happening. He tried to remember the things he had learned in one of those training classes he had taken for self-defense. But his mind went blank feeling the coldness of gun against his head and he began to panic. "Please, I have money, I can…" he said all jumpy before being cut off.

"Get in the car," Dayvid commanded again this time a little more stern as he pressed the gun harder against the man's neck. He chuckled to himself unable to believe that Rain had chosen this scary ass cracker as their lawyer. *She had to plan on killing this muthafucka when it was all over,"* he thought to himself watching the fidgety lawyer. Morganstein was in just as deep as the Porters. He had been assisting the fugitive family the entire time the sisters had been on the run, so going to the feds would land him in just as much trouble.

Morganstein cautiously slid into the front seat as Dayvid got into the backseat directly behind him, all while keeping the gun trained on him. Dayvid finally pulled the hood off his head revealing himself and lowered his weapon easing the man's fears.

"Oh my god, Dayvid," a shocked Morganstein said looking in his rearview mirror like he saw a ghost. "I thought you were dead," he said continuing to face forward like no one was in the car with him.

"Good, hopefully everyone is just as convinced as you," Dayvid replied.

"How in the hell did you…" the lawyer asked before being cut off again.

"That's not important right now, but what is, is that money that Rain gave you," Dayvid expressed.

"I have it, I can get it to you. Can you meet me here this time tomorrow?"

"Nah, I don't have that type of time. I need it like ASAP," he explained.

"I can meet you back here in a few hours. When all the offices are closed and it's not so busy." Morganstein offered.

"Ok," Dayvid replied. "Did you take care of that other thing I asked you to do?"

"Yes."

"Good."

"Hey man, I'm sorry about Rain," the lawyer said in a somber tone.

"Yeah, thanks," Dayvid said playing along. "9 o'clock, top level," he continued as he hopped out the vehicle.

"Ok," Morganstein answered but Dayvid was gone just as fast as he appeared.

Dayvid checked his watch, Morganstein should have been pulling up at any moment. By force of habit Dayvid had shown up 30 minutes early and scoped out the scene. After all he was still dealing with a lawyer, most of them were slimy and he wouldn't put anything past Morganstein. Another 5 minutes past when Dayvid saw the lawyer's Mercedes pull onto the roof level of the parking garage and circle the parking lot once before pulling into a parking space across from him. Dayvid saw the headlights on the Mercedes flash, so he flashed his back then exited the Acura and made his way over to the lawyer's car. Halfway between his car and Morganstein's, three of the doors on the Mercedes popped open and three armed men dressed in t-shirts and jeans spilled out and began firing at Dayvid.

"Oh shit," Dayvid said as he quickly pivoted while pulling his Ruger out of his hoodie and firing off shots as he raced behind a parked car for cover. He crouched down with his back pressed up against the side of a car as he caught his breath from the shock. Morganstein never planned on turning over that money and had sent a hit squad that was quickly bearing down on Dayvid as he fired back trying to keep them at bay. Dayvid moved around the back of the car before popping up and hitting one of the men in the chest dropping him. Ducking back out of sight as bullets whizzed all around, shattering the glass of the car he was hiding behind causing it to rain down on him. Dayvid moved cautiously between cars positioning himself behind another. He came up shooting again but hit nothing and had to dodge a bullet coming back at him. Becoming frustrated, Dayvid rolled underneath a car trying to determine the shooters exact whereabouts and could see them racing towards the car he was under. He could hear the two men communicating with one another trying to locate him.

"Where the fuck did he go?" one said to the other.

"I don't fucking know," the other answered. "Go around that way."

Dayvid watched as the men circled the car before firing a shot, hitting one of them in the ankle. He dropped to the pavement screaming in pain. The other man seeing the shot come from under the car began firing wildly at the ground underneath the car. After a while he stopped when he didn't hear any shots being returned. Slowly, he crept closer to the car and crotched down trying to see if he had finished their target off. But looking under the car, Dayvid was nowhere to be found.

"Fuck," the man said banging his hand on the ground before getting to his feet.

Dayvid already had the drop on him though, standing on the other side of the car with his gun raised. He fired three times.

The man's chest exploded into a bloody mess as all three shots entered his flesh dropping him. Dayvid circled the car, were the man he had shot in the ankle laid writhing in pain. He kicked the man's gun out of his reach, then stepped on his ankle causing the man to scream in agony. "Where's Morganstein?" Dayvid asked.

"I don't know no Morganstein," the man said through pain.

Dayvid shot him in both knees before asking him again. "Where can I find Morganstein?"

"414 Water Street," the man confessed.

Dayvid didn't respond, he just fired a shot into the man's

forehead killing him.

* * *

Alan Morganstein paced back and forth on the balcony of his luxurious condo located on the inner harbor. Checking his phone every few minutes, the call he had been waiting on should have come over an hour ago. His appearance was disheveled, his partially buttoned light blue dress shirt was marked by sweat stains and was half tucked into his pants. His hair was out of place and his eyes were as wide as an interstate. Unable to keep still, the high grade of cocaine running through his veins only increased his paranoia. Morganstein was in way over his head and he knew it, he had used the Porters' money to pay on a debt he owed to Russian mobsters for his cocaine and gambling habits. He had been using their money to place bets and for the most part he had been lucky, but his drug use had become more prevalent and he had hit an unlucky streak. He thought his luck had turned around after he saw Rain's death on the news. He planned on botching Dayvid's case and never having to answer for the money he had stolen. His plan seemed to work better than he had thought after reports began to surface of Dayvid's apparent suicide. But his resurrection from the dead had thrown a wrench in his scheme and he needed to get rid of Dayvid, after all he was assumed dead already. The drugs and his fear had the lawyer thinking irrational, that was why he had convinced a few of his coke sniffing buddies to ambush an unsuspecting Dayvid. A choice he was now second guessing as he continued to wait for his phone to ring.

"That's what I get for using amateurs," he said to himself. His nerves were truly getting the best of him and so was his craving for more of the drug. Morganstein re-entered the condo and raced over to his glass coffee table that had about 6 grams of coke on it. He used the credit card next to the white powder to chop it up and separate two lines before using a cut straw to snort a line in one nostril and another into the other nostril. He threw his head back and closed his eyes enjoying the drip of the drug in the back of his throat and for a brief moment all of his worries disappeared.

"This a nice spot you got here."

Morganstein was shaken from his trance by the voice in his living room. He opened his eyes to see Dayvid Porter sitting in a chair in the corner with a gun pointed directly at him.

"Dayvid," he said as his high immediately was blown and fear began to fill his body. "Let me explain…"

"No need," Dayvid said interrupting him, not one for the long drawn out talk. He was going to kill Morganstein and both of them knew it. The lawyer had sent men to kill a killer and they had missed signing his own death certificate. Dayvid only had one question. "Where's my money?"

"It's gone," Morganstein said in a slight whimper. "I used it to pay some Russians I owed. But I can…"

The sound of the gunshots drowned out the end of the lawyer's explanation and the two shots in the chest stopped him mid-sentence, jerking his body back on the couch. The large amount of cocaine running through his body wouldn't let Morganstein die immediately. His chest just heaved up and down as blood began to leak from his mouth. His lips moved like he was trying to speak but no sound came out. Dayvid stood up from the chair and walked over to where the lawyer laid dying on the couch and squeezed another round into the middle of his head. Dayvid tucked the gun into his sweatpants, put his hood over his head and quickly exited the condo. Once out in the hallway Dayvid pulled the fire alarm and blended in with the residents as they exited the building. He overheard a young couple telling another couple that they think they had heard gunshots as he passed them and disappeared around the corner as he heard sirens in the distance.

6

His instructions were plain enough: "... Spare nothing from the sword." *-1 Samuel 15:3*

A Month Later

The footsteps above him along with the rapping of the latest Meek Mill's song let Dayvid know there was only one lookout on the porch of the dope spot. Probably the same young lookout with the headphones around his neck that he had saw for the past few nights patrolling the front door. He had been laying on the spot for over a week, watching the hoppers, the fiends and all comings and goings and saw that it was making its fair share of money. Dayvid had become a mercenary, hitting spots all over city in order to stay afloat, while he searched for Nova and plotted another big score that could get him the funds he needed to get to Mexico. So far both had come up empty. Nova was nowhere to be found. Everywhere Dayvid thought she may have settled down turned out to be a dead end. He knew Baltimore was all she had ever known, it was her comfort zone and most likely Nova wouldn't have strayed too far away. But as the days turned to weeks, he was starting to think she had left Maryland for good and like the rest of the world she was under the assumption he was dead. That's what made it imperative that he hit a big lick and get out of dodge, it was becoming increasingly harder to remain out of sight when he needed to come out and get money.

Dayvid took a deep breath and pulled the mask down over his face while holding his Desert Eagle close to his chest. The nervousness he once felt as a young teen had long disappeared. You had to have nerves of steel in his line of work and Dayvid Porter had them in spades. Popping up from his hiding spot under the porch steps, Dayvid caught the unsuspecting lookout by surprise. The big gun in his face caused the young man's heart to skip a beat, making him lose control of his bladder and pissing himself. Dayvid laughed to himself as he knocked the boy's headphones off his head and reached in his waist looking for a gun but found none.

They got this lil' nigga out here with no strap, stupid muthafuckas, Dayvid thought to himself. "How many niggas inside?" he asked while pressing his gun against the young man's forehead.

"Two," the young man said fighting back tears. He was clearly not built for this life.

Dayvid grabbed him by the back of the neck and pushed him towards the door. "You better get that door open," he demanded.

The young man in fear for his life was willing to do whatever he was asked, if it meant staying alive. He knocked on the door of the spot in a rhythm only known to the men inside. A few seconds later the door opened and a short, brown stocky man stood in the door with his gun tucked in his waist but showing.

"What you want nigga, I told your lil' dumb ass to stay on the porch and keep a look out," the man chastised the youngster. "What the fuck is wrong wit' you?" he asked noticing the look on his face.

Dayvid suddenly appeared in the door with his gun trained on the man, who instinctively reached for his weapon. The loud bark of the Desert Eagle shook the house and echoed throughout the block. The bullet hit the man in the chest lifting him off his feet, sending him backwards into the house. Dayvid pushed the young hopper into the house, using him as a shield while holding the gun to his head. The youngster's ears were still ringing from the shot being fired. A tall, dark, slim man raced out from another room with his gun drawn but hesitated seeing Dayvid holding the young hustler in the line of fire and his man lying on the floor dead. His indecision was costly as Dayvid fired a shot at him barley missing, causing him to drop his weapon and raise his hands in surrender.

"No disrespect my nigga, but do you know who spot you

robbing?" he asked hoping that would change the masked man's mind.

"Nah and I don't give a fuck. Now drop that bag off?" Dayvid shouted referring to the black garbage bag on the table behind him. The man did as he was told, retrieving the bag and dropping it at Dayvid's feet before being made to join the young lookout, who was already stretched out on the floor. Dayvid scooped the bag up, looked inside to verify it was cash then dipped out the door.

Dayvid dashed down the alley on the side of the house that led to the next block, where he had stashed his getaway car. He threw the bag into the front seat and jumped in the car, just as two police cars came racing down the block with their lights on and sirens blaring. Dayvid quickly removed his mask, put his hat on his head pulling it down low and laying his seat back as they passed. His appearance had changed drastically as of late, he was sporting a full beard and a curly afro that were both unkempt making him unrecognizable but he still wasn't taking any chances. Dayvid had never been overly concerned with his looks, he was naturally a fly dude. The old adage *"Clothes don't make the man"* fit Dayvid Porter to a tee. He looked good in whatever he put on without much effort but looking good was the furthest thing from his mind. He was in beast mode and any and everybody was on the menu. He watched as a few more patrol cars zoomed pass then pulled out heading back to his hide out.

Dayvid parked the Acura a block over like usual and cut

through the wooded path heading for the fence that led to the backyard of the basement hideout. Moving rapidly through the cut, his adrenaline was still pumping from the rush of the robbery as the bag swung in one hand and he held his gun tightly in the other. His mind was focused solely on counting his take, he could tell by the weight of the bag that it wasn't as much as he hoped and he was already thinking of his next play. Dayvid's mind automatically began to bounce ideas around when a sudden noise startled him and a man popped out of the bushes behind him. He turned in time to see the man raising his hand with something in it. Dayvid reacted quickly lifting his weapon and firing twice hitting the man with both shots. Dayvid froze in shock seeing the man crumble to the ground, as he got a clear look and realized it was just a homeless man with a soda bottle in his hand.

"Aw shit," Dayvid voiced realizing what he had just done. Although he was no stranger to committing murder, he had never killed an innocent person or someone who didn't deserve it. He stared down at the dead man as he filled up with guilt. Dayvid was moving recklessly and he was wound up tight. *Damn I'm lunchin'*, he said to himself. Looking around to see if anyone had saw what he had done, he realized the view to the path was obscured by all the greenery. With no other choice he grabbed the man by his arms and drug him back into the bushes trying to hide his body but he knew it wouldn't be long before someone stumbled upon the dead man or he started stinking, either way it wasn't good. Dayvid immediately made up his mind he wouldn't be around when that happened.

The hideout was now too hot to take a chance staying there and it would not be long before cops were crawling all over the block. Dayvid hopped the fence and quickly disappeared into the apartment before reemerging a few seconds later with a duffle bag over his shoulder. He threw his hood over his head and began his trek up the block in search of a new spot to hide out. Dayvid remembered an extended stay motel off of I-695 that took cash and asked no questions. It was filled with mostly welfare recipients and drug addicts, it was also right by the highway, just in case he needed to make a quick escape. Dayvid decided to ditch his hoopty, in favor of the MTA light rail, it had served its purpose. He had another car stashed in a garage in Essex that he planned on using from now on. Slipping into the MTA station at Franklin and Warwick, he boarded an eastbound train for Old Eastern and Back River Neck in route to the Super 8 on Stemmers Run Rd.

The motel sign was dimly lit and looked as if it could go out at any minute as Dayvid strolled through the parking lot and into the rundown spot's office. After a few minutes he exited with a key to his room on the second floor. Ascending the steps, he was greeted by two fiends engaged in an argument as soon as he reached the top. The drug addicted couple ignored his presence and continued their shouting match as Dayvid walked around them. After a few more steps, he stood in front of the door that read 225. He entered the room and clicked the switch letting the door close behind him. A few roaches ran for cover as the room lit up and a couple bold ones didn't move at all. Dayvid tossed his bag on the chair and began looking around at the room. He almost wished he had left the lights off, but it would have to do. He removed the gun from his waist sitting it on the nightstand next to the bed before sitting down on the side of the bed and immediately began contemplating his next move.

7

"He gives power to the faint; and to them that have no might he increases strength." *-Isaiah 40:29*

Nova had long lost track of what day it was, the date and time hadn't mattered much since the news of Dayvid's death shattered her world. Wearied by her constant crying, she blacked out the entire room and slept for days at a time, hoping the pain would eventually subside. She had gone through the chain of emotions and had come to the conclusion that the emptiness she felt would never really go away. A love that strong wasn't easy to let go, forgotten or thrown by the wayside. Laying in the plush king-sized bed, flipping through channels had become commonplace for her but she knew that she couldn't hide from the world forever. The night of his death she balled up on the floor and cried for him, contemplating suicide herself, wanting nothing more than to join him in the afterlife. But her better judgment prevailed and although she had decided against taking her own life, she hadn't really decided to live either.

Nova for some reason felt different this morning. Today she had awakened with vigor and a renewed sense of hope. Tired of staring at the four walls of her somber hotel room, she wanted to get out and pamper herself. Feeling as though she had neglected herself long enough, Nova located a hair salon and spa in walking distance of the hotel. She also planned on doing a little retail therapy while she was at it. After a hot shower Nova threw on some tights and a t-shirt along with a pair of sneakers. Putting her hair up in bun, she took a stack of cash from the safe and stuffed it in her bag. Nova was indecisive if leaving all the cash in the room was a good idea but she also knew carrying it all on her wasn't smart either. Checking herself one last time, she smiled then headed out the door to start her day.

The few hours spent in the chair seemed well worth as the stylist spun Nova around allowing her to admire herself in the mirror. The wide smile on her face answered the hair stylist's question before she could even ask and left no doubt in her mind that her client was pleased. Nova loved her new look, a curly, medium bob with side swept bangs and blonde highlights. She felt beautiful again and sprung from the chair full of energy like a school kid when the bell rings. She paid the woman making sure to tip to show her appreciate then exited out the door in search of a boutique on 14th Street the hairdresser had told her about. Shopping was definitely Nova's favorite pastime, she found peace in the alone time, it was therapeutic for her. She could lose herself for hours at a time just trying and buying as she called it and today she needed it more than ever before.

Sashaying out the boutique with two hands filled with bags, the pep had returned to Nova's strut. Confidence was something she had never lacked but the bruises on her heart were deep and her crushed spirit needed repairing. Although she hadn't fully returned to her normal self, by the roar coming from her stomach it was clear that her appetite had returned. Nova had grown tired of the food at the hotel and was in no rush to return to her lifeless room she had occupied for the past six weeks. So, when she came across the Pearl Dive Oyster Palace she didn't hesitate to enter.

The boardwalk themed seafood restaurant and bar had a rustic décor that showcased a variety of repurposed items from around the country. The southern hospitality feeling of the place welcomed Nova upon entering and she was quickly seated at a table a few feet from the bar. It had been a while since she was in a social setting and looking around the room at the mixed after work crowd Nova began to realize how much she missed it. She entertained herself briefly watching the other patrons mingle and sharing laughs with one another while waiting on the glass of wine she ordered. When her waitress returned Nova asked for more time to go over the menu and the young lady gladly obliged. As her eyes canvassed the menu she couldn't help but feel like someone was watching her every move. Peeking up from the menu, Nova noticed a handsome, caramel complexion gentleman leaning on the bar dressed in a grey fitted V-neck sweater that hugged his slim athletic frame, showing off his well-built body. His True Religion jeans and loosely laced timberlands gave him a bit of edge and complemented his otherwise clean cut look. His sleeves were rolled up showing off the nice gold watch he wore on his wrist. Nova was mesmerized by his brown eyes that stared so intently into her own not allowing her to turn away.

Watching him stride across the room towards her, holding a drink in his hand, she thought to herself how the closer he got the better he looked. Nova returned her eyes to the menu in front of her, pretending she didn't see him coming.

When Charles St. Clair saw her, he recognized her immediately. Though he didn't know her name and couldn't place her face, he knew the beautiful woman looked familiar.

"Eating alone?"

Nova looked up allowing their eyes to meet again. "Yes...I am."

Saint smiled at her. "Would you mind if I joined you?"

His dazzling smile was persuasive, almost irresistible making Nova consider his offer more than she normally would have. But she really was in no mood for company, especially of the opposite sex.

"Sorry, but I'm gonna have to decline," Nova shook her head

with a smile, trying to lighten the blow of rejection. "But thanks for the offer."

"No problem ma, can't blame me for tryin' tho," he said taking it surprisingly well.

Nova could tell he wasn't the type of nigga that heard no a lot. He could probably pull out his phone, scroll his call log and find a willing piece of pussy with ease. Fact was he was a fly, sexy nigga Nova had to admit to herself.

"Well can I get a name to match the face?" he asked. "At least I could take that with me on this walk of shame back to the bar," he said with a smile.

Nova smiled back finding him very charming. "Renee," she lied only willing to give her fake name.

"I'm Charles. But everybody calls me Saint," he said. "Nice to meet you ma, I'm gonna let you get back to your menu tho. You might wanna try the BBQ shrimp, they're bangin'."

"Thank you," she nodded at his suggestion. "Nice meeting you too."

Nova sat alone enjoying her shrimp, Saint had been right, they were bangin' and they went well with her second glass of Moscato. Finishing up, she was now ready to head back to her room and enjoy a hot bubble bath while winding down. She smiled seeing her waitress heading her way, happy she wouldn't have to wait long for the check.

"You ready for dessert?" the bubbly young lady asked with a

smile on her face.

"No," Nova waved her off with a smile. "But I am ready for the check."

"You're good ma'am," the waitress said.

A confused Nova just stared. "Excuse me?"

"Your bill has been taken care of already," she paused to turning around. "By the gentleman over there," she said pointing to Saint at the bar.

When Nova made eye contact with him, Saint just raised his glass, smiled and nodded. Nova smiled back, said thank you and headed out the door.

She hadn't made it halfway up the block when she heard Saint calling her name from behind.

"Renee! Excuse me, Renee!" he yelled.

It took him calling her a second time for it to register that he was talking to her. *Damn just when I thought this nigga was cool. I ain't for the stalker shit,* she thought to herself as she turned to see what he wanted. But to her surprise Saint stood there holding all her shopping bags in his hands.

"You forgot something ma," he charmingly said walking up on her.

"Oh my God," Nova said dumbfounded. "Thank you so much, I can't believe I did that. You're a life saver," she said hugging him.

"Yeah, this would have fucked your night up. We can't have that," he said lifting the bags seeing that see had spent a nice bit of bread. "These bags a lil' heavy, let me carry 'em to ya car for you."

"It's ok, I didn't drive but I'm just up the block. I'll be alright," she insisted.

"At least let me walk you then. You don't need to be carrying all these bags out here by yourself. It's getting dark."

Nova thought about it for a second then agreed. She really didn't feel like carrying those bags any longer anyway, plus she appreciated the chivalry. The two walked the short distance to the hotel exchanging small talk on the way. Nova found out Saint was originally from New York but now lived in Baltimore and he was only in DC on business for the weekend. She didn't divulge too much information about herself, only that she had just moved to DC and she was staying at the hotel until she found an apartment. A lie because she hadn't made up her mind as to where she was going to settle down. Standing in front of the hotel, Nova was still feeling grateful that he had noticed she left her bags.

"Thanks again, I can't thank you enough," Nova said.

"You could let me take you out to dinner tomorrow night," Saint said smoothly staring into her as he clasped her hand in his.

"Dinner?" she asked giving him the side eye jokingly. "I don't know."

"It's just food ma, I ain't asking for your hand in marriage," he teased.

"Ok." She accepted giving in to those mesmerizing eyes of his.

"What's your number?" Saint asked pulling out his phone

before Nova ran off the numbers quickly. "Ok that's me calling you, lock me in," he said, handing her the bags and stood in front of the hotel until he saw her disappear onto the elevator.

Entering her room Nova dropped her bags down. She was happy to see it was clean like the day she first checked in. Room service had come in and made the luxurious room beautiful again, sort of like she had done herself during the day. It seemed fitting. Her mind immediately went to the money in the safe. Racing over to the safe, her heart pounded in her chest but Nova felt relieved when she saw the money hadn't been touched. Walking into the bathroom she began running the water for her bath then returned to the room, removing her phone from her handbag. Staring at the number from her last missed call she thought about deleting it but after a few minutes she typed Saint's name in and pressed save.

* * *

U.S Marshal Torrence and Palmeri sat in the unmarked car across the street from The DuPont Circle Hotel snapping pictures of the woman they now knew as Renee Preston. They had gotten her name and room number from the desk clerk at the hotel and had been dying to lay their eyes on her. The woman who had been staying in the hotel for almost 2 months paying cash for a room that she never left and was now on their radar. The serial numbers on some of the cash had been red flagged in the system, meaning it had been marked from a bank robbery almost a year and a half ago. A robbery committed by the infamous Porter clan and the two Marshals had been following her all day in hopes she would lead them to one of the remaining Porters still at large. Torrence was obsessed with closing this case and even though Rain and Dayvid were now dead she wouldn't rest until she slapped cuffs on Fallon and Autumn. The Porters trail had gone cold after Rain's death but Torrence felt she had just found her new lead. She didn't know how the woman was connected but her gut told her she was definitely connected and she wasn't going to stop until she found out how.

"Who do you think she is?" Palmeri asked his partner.

"I don't know but I just have this feeling she's connected some kind of way," Torrence expressed passionately.

"It's been almost two years since that robbery. That money could have passed through so many hands by now," Palmeri explained. "What makes you so sure she's connected? She has no record whatsoever it's almost like she doesn't exist."

"Exactly," she said at him making her point for her.

The Porters were the biggest case of her career, hell they were the biggest thing in her life at the moment. She had sacrificed her home life in favor of her job and it had cost her the family she built. Bringing the Porters down would make it all worth it to her.

"Just a feeling that's all. What's she hiding or who is she hiding from, is what I wanna know?" Torrence continued. "She's been staying at this hotel for over a month and had never left her room not one time until today. That's not normal."

Palmeri nodded his head agreeing. "You have a point. What about the guy with her?"

"Probably a nobody, but snap a few of him, just in case." Torrence instructed.

* * *

Flowing from the hotel dressed in a split-neck, red sheath dress with an exposed front zipper and Christian Louboutin zebra stripe platform pumps, every head turned to get a look at Nova as she pranced towards the waiting vehicle. Saint stood holding the door of his pearl white 750 BMW open with a wide smile across his face. Dressed in a black Alexander McQueen zip shoulder sweatshirt, matching jeans and Balenciaga sneakers with a gold Cuban link laying on his chest he was definitely easy on the eyes. Something Nova took notice of as she spoke before getting into the car.

"You look nice."

"So, do you, smell good too," Saint said taking in her intoxicating smell as she past. He was feeling her fashion sense and admiring her curves at the same time. *Damn, her fly match my fly. It's something about this broad I like,* he thought to himself closing the car door behind her.

Saint escorted Nova into Charlie Palmer's, a stylish steakhouse located on Constitution Ave. He had reserved a table on the rooftop terrace with a remarkable view of the Capitol Building. Admittedly impressed, Nova took a long look while Saint pulled her chair out and waited for her to be seated.

"You like it?" he asked already knowing the answer but still wanting to hear her say it.

"Yeah, this is nice," she affirmed.

"I'm glad you like it. I got something special planned for you," he said with a smirk on his face.

"Is that right?" she questioned with a suspicious look wondering what he was up to.

"Yeah, I picked this place for a reason. Not only is the food good but it houses the biggest wine cube in the city; 6,000 bottles over 500 different selections. I noticed your affinity for wine and thought I would set up a wine tasting," Saint revealed.

"Affinity," Nova teased but admiring his choice of words. She knew he was a street nigga by the way he moved but could tell he wasn't the average, run of the mill type. She had been schooled by one of the most thorough niggas the streets had ever seen and knew how to read most men. Dayvid had always been honest with her about the things he did, at least as honest as he could be without putting her in harm's way. He equipped her with the same ability he had of studying people, read their true intentions and learn how they think so she could know their moves before they made them.

"Damn you hard on a nigga ma," Saint stated jokingly. "What you wanna start with?" he asked passing her the wine menu.

Nova picked a half of dozen wines to taste off the menu, then the two began getting to know each other better while they waited.

"So tell me more about yourself?" Saint asked.

"Not much to tell, I'm not that exciting, just regular ol' me," she spoke continuing to play it close to the vest with the handsome stranger.

"There's nothing regular about you," he said in his smooth, husky tone. "At least not from where I'm sitting."

Nova blushed, every woman love compliments and she was no different. She had never been out on a date with no man other than Dayvid and was feeling a little tense. Saint could sense her reservation and was doing his best to make her comfortable. He could tell she was holding back but instead of pressing her, he keep the conversation light and flowing as the waiter began filling their table up with the different wines.

"So how's the apartment search going?" he asked.

"Hmm," Nova said caught off guard before quickly remembering what she had told him. "It's going, I should settle on something soon," she played along in between sips of wine.

"I can help, if you like. I know a couple real estate agents, I could make few a calls. I could come back out here next weekend and we can go check out a few of my people's spots."

"You're mighty confident. Let's see how this date goes first before you start planning another," she teased him again.

"Haha!" he said throwing his head back enjoying the laugh. "You really on some shit, ain't chu?"

Nova's slick mouth and quick wit was right up his alley, she reminded him of the women back in his home state of New York. The more she put up a fight the more he liked her. He appreciated a good challenge, most woman fell all over themselves around him, creaming their panties with thoughts of fucking him. Those women tend to end up in the graveyard of his memory, never receiving a call back and easily forgotten. The woman he knew only as Renee intrigued him and definitely had his full attention.

"So what is it that you do?" she asked assuming he was in the dope game but knowing if he was he wouldn't tell. At least not if he was a real nigga. Real niggas didn't flaunt their business; they actually did the opposite, flew under the radar and continued getting money on the low.

"I own a record label with a partner of mine. I'm out here trying to sign an R&B artist. I have to meet with her manager tomorrow before I leave," he offered the half-truth. Fact was he came to DC twice a month to meet up with his connect and planned on taking a few bricks back to Baltimore with him.

"Is she any good?" Nova asked.

"Yeah, she's dope. Maybe you can check her out sometimes. I'm thinking about putting a little showcase together for her. That's if I can sign her," he explained.

Nova was a big music fan, so that definitely sounded like something she would be down for. She didn't know if it was the glasses of wine or his charm and sexy smile that had her considering seeing him again, but she was. Now she was just hoping he didn't do or say anything that would ruin those thoughts.

After a few hours of talking, eating and plenty of drinking, Nova had definitely began to feel the effects from all the wine tasting. She was tipsy and knew her limit. Saint felt it too. Not much of a wine consumer he had underestimated the libation.

"Yo I'm a little nice," he admitted sliding his chair back and stumbling slightly getting to his feet.

"Rookie," Nova mockingly teased enjoying a laugh at his expense. But the joke was quickly on her as she stumbled getting to her feet as well causing them both to burst into laughter.

Saint reached in his pocket pulling out a knot, peeling off two hundreds he tossed them on the table figuring that would more than cover the bill and the tip. Putting his arm out, Nova interlocked hers with his and they proceeded to walk out the restaurant arm in arm, using one another for balance in order not to look as drunk they were. Exiting the steakhouse into the cool night air, the draft hit Nova immediately sending a chill through her body. Saint placed his arm around her hoping to warm her up as best as he could while they headed towards his car. The air had seemed to elevate the effects of the wine in their system giving them both rubbery legs.

"Yo I'ma get a fucking ticket," Saint slurred as he navigated his car through the streets of DC trying to get Nova back to the hotel without crashing or getting pulled over.

"You should have let me drive like I said," she responded.

"You right, shit we almost there now."

Pulling up to the hotel, Nova was relieved they made it safely, but staring at Saint she could tell he was in no condition to be driving. She had enjoyed her evening and would truly feel guilty if something was to happen to him leaving her hotel in route to his final destination.

"Don't take this the wrong way," she started with a disclaimer. "But you're in no shape to be driving anywhere. So you're more than welcome to come upstairs and crash…on the couch…in the living room."

Saint appreciated the offer and after initially declining he reconsidered, accepting after some persuading.

"On the couch…in the living room," Nova reiterated before they exited the car and headed upstairs.

They both staggered into the room but Saint was clearly drunker than her. She warned him at dinner about throwing back those glasses of wine like they were juice but he refused to listen and now the room felt like a carousel spinning with him on it.

"This a nice spot," he mumbled admiring the luxe hotel room while making his way to the couch and plopping down.

"Yeah," she answered still finding humor in his drunkenness. "I'm gonna get you a pillow," she said disappearing into the bedroom. Returning quickly, she was greeted by the sound of his light snoring and him stretched out. Nova just stared in the doorway looking at him shaking her head. *Rookie*, she thought to herself then went back in her room and got an extra blanket out the closet. She approached a passed out Saint on the couch and like she had done plenty of times for Dayvid, she removed his sneakers, placed the pillow under his head and covered him with the blanket. He looked comfortable to her and she left him to his sleep. Nova entered the bedroom, closing and locking the door behind her. Kicking off her heels and slipping out her dress, she climbed into bed and drifted off to sleep.

The sound of banging on the front door of the room, woke her and the sun glaring through the curtains made her squint her eyes as she opened them. Nova rolled out of bed and head to the closet quickly putting on a pair of workout pants and a t-shirt then unlocked the bedroom door and walked out into the living room area. Conspicuous by his absence, Saint was nowhere to be found. The blanket she had covered him with was neatly folded on the couch with the pillow on top of it. Other than that, there were no traces that he had even been there.

"Was it too much to say bye or thank you," Nova said to aloud to herself as she continued to the door. "Who is it," she called out.

"It's me," a voice from the other side replied. "Saint."

Nova opened the door and there he stood with bags of breakfast in his hand. "I just wanted to show my appreciation for letting me crash," he said smoothly.

A smile crept across her face as she stepped aside and let him in.

"I didn't know what you liked so I got a bunch of different shit. I got coffee & orange juice too," he said holding out the cup holder with four cups in it. "Which one you like?"

"Coffee," she answered gliding across the room joining him on the couch.

Both of them were starving, ravaging the food in no time. After letting her food settle, Nova jumped up and began to gather the trash and walked across the suite to discard it. Saint stared at her nice round ass protruding in the workout pants she wore and felt himself getting slightly aroused. The feeling heightened as she turned to face him and he got a glimpse of her pussy print.

Fuck a camel toe, that shit fat as an elephant's foot, he thought to himself. "I gotta get ready to go. I got that meeting," he said as if he was reminding himself. Truthfully, he didn't have to or want to go just yet but didn't want to linger around too long. He would rather leave on his own terms instead of being asked to; never the one to overstay his welcome. He stood up and caught her eyes briefly drift down to the bulge that had formed in his pants before looking him in the face again.

"I really enjoyed myself," she said following him to the door.

"Me too, hopefully we can do this again real soon," he said opening the door.

"Yeah that would be nice," she replied leaning in for a hug.

"I'm gonna call you," he answered and pulled her into his embrace.

Nova liked the way he felt hugging her, she could feel his bulge as she pressed against his body, sending a warm tingling sensation through her panties. Instinctively, Nova kissed him and Saint indulged, slipping his tongue into her mouth allowing the two to dance with each other momentarily before they separated.

"Yeah, make sure you do that," she said with a smile. "Bye," she said before pushing him out the door and closing it.

Saint just smiled and shook his head.

8

"Perhaps I am his enemy, but he can never be mine." –*King David*

(The Bible)

The flashing lights of cop cars had become a normal occurrence at the rundown motel, infested with as many drug addicts as roaches. Screaming and yelling quickly escalated into physical altercations when drugs were involved. Tonight, a prostitute had robbed a trick and he had returned with the cops. Dayvid peered through the curtains and watched the whole scene play out waiting patiently for the cops to clear out. When the coast was clear, he cracked open the door of the room, looking both ways out onto the balcony, before pulling his hat down and his hood over his head. He had been living off of sodas and snacks out the vending machine but every trip was an adventure trying to remain as low key as possible. Even though most of the residents were probably oblivious to who he was and what was going on with him.

Dayvid descended the steps moving towards the vending machines with his hand tuck in his jacket, not far from his gun. He pulled a few dollars out his pocket, straightening them and putting them in the machine to make his choice when he heard a voice.

"Hey mister," said the tiny voice coming from his right.

Dayvid turned seeing a tattered, little, brown skinned girl looking up at him with a baby face and puppy dog eyes. Her hair was a mess and she was in need of several baths; typical of the kids staying at the hotel.

"Hi," she said with a cute snaggletooth smile once she had his attention. "Whatchu doing?" she asked rocking back and forth.

"Getting something to eat," he replied.

"I'm hungry too," she said. "Can you buy me something?"

Dayvid could tell by looking at the little girl that she wasn't eating the way she should and wasn't being looked after properly due to the fact that she was roaming around the unsavory place at night unattended. Her round little face, brown skin and big eyes rang so familiar to him. Even through the raggedy appearance reminded him of Fallon when she was younger and she would burst into his room begging from him to take her to the store. He couldn't resist Fallon then and he couldn't resist the little girl standing in front of him now.

"Of course," he said. "What you want?" he asked moving aside so she could get a look.

"Keyara!" a woman's voice could be heard yelling. "Where your lil' ass at? Keyara!"

The look on the little girl's face let Dayvid know those screams were for her.

"What are you doing?" the woman chastised as she turned the corner seeing her daughter. "I'ma beat your little ass," she threatened.

Dayvid looked the woman up and down, her appearance screamed addict. By the tracks in her arms and her constant scratching, it was obvious her drug of choice. Dope made zombies of out of its users, the infected sores it left up and down their arms and legs from dirty needles made them look like the walking dead.

"Hi, how are you?" she asked looking up at the mysterious, handsome stranger standing in front of her, trying to sound sexy.

"I'm good," he replied meaning it in every way possible. "And she's good," he continued referring to Keyara. "I was just about to get her something out the vending machine that's all."

"What I told you about begging?" the woman slapped the girl in the back of the head.

"No, she didn't ask, I offered," he said trying to save the little one. "I was getting something and she was standing there, so I asked."

"Oh, a gentleman. I like that," the woman said eyeing him up and down. "Maybe me and you can work out something," she propositioned willing to do anything to score her next fix.

"Oh nah, I'm good," Dayvid quickly answered.

The woman, seeing Dayvid was not interested, tried a different approach. "Maybe you're interested in something else," she replied placing her hand on her young daughter and nudging her forward.

Fire quickly rose in Dayvid's belly hearing the woman offer her young daughter to him. He grabbed the woman and pushed her up against the wall. "What the fuck is wrong witchu? I look like I like little girls to you bitch. What kind of mother are you?" he said pressing the gun under her chin.

"Mommy!" the young girl screamed.

Causing him to turn and look at her, the fear in her eyes made him loosen his grip. "Get your shit together," he growled before turning and handing Keyara the snacks he bought for her and walking away as she stared at him.

* * *

Dayvid stood hidden in the shadows near the dumpster by the back door of the club and waited patiently for it to open. Tired of hitting little spots for odds and ends, he was ready for a bigger score. But with a bigger score, came bigger risk. The Porters had hit most, if not all of the big time hustlers in the city, but that was as a team. Dayvid knew a lot of niggas had hired reinforcements after falling victim and his chances of pulling off those jobs the second time around without his sisters were slim to none. So it was back to being a stick up artist and doing kick door robberies, something that wasn't foreign to him. He and Rain had pulled tons of home invasions in their early days, before Smitty helped hone their skills and they decided to involve their younger sisters in the family business.

Routinely, the female bartenders would step out the back door to smoke their cigarettes. Dayvid knew that was his way in. All he had to do was bide his time.

The vibrating bass of the loud music could be felt all the way in the dimly lit back office of the hole in the wall club. A thick cloud of smoke and the loud smell of weed filled the air as Pharaoh and two of his niggas sat around a folding leg card table counting money. Pharaoh, a big belly, dark skinned, grimy looking nigga with dreads ran the strip club; which rarely had patrons and basically served as a hangout for his crew of corner boys. All the strippers that worked at the club were part of his stable of bitches that sold their pussy for him. They did more fucking than dancing, whether it was with customers in the VIP areas or Pharaoh and his niggas. Which lead to the spot being nicknamed "The Ho Depot." Those in the knowing, knew it was also the place to cop if you were a hustler in the city. Pharaoh had set up shop in South Baltimore a few months ago and started moving bricks seemingly out of nowhere. No one knew how the former corner boy had suddenly bossed up but what was clear was that he was getting it.

"Nigga I'm telling you, I had both dem bitches in the telly turnt up," Pharaoh said between tokes of the weed, in his deep, husky voice. He spoke as if his tongue was too heavy for his mouth. "They was on the molly, had em sucking dick, eating pussy, playin in each other ass, all that shit," he said exhaling smoke and laughing.

"Yo, ain't one of them little broads KP from West Baltimore sister?" one of the men asked.

"I look like I give a fuck? Little bitch gotta fat ass," Pharaoh boasted. "That nigga KP a pussy. He wouldn't bust a grape in a fruit fight," he said passing the weed. "I gotta piss," he announced rising to his feet, removing the gun from his waist and placing it down on the table. "Yo, watch this nigga here," he jokingly instructing one of the men while pointing at the other.

Pharaoh stood over the toilet relieving himself. The sound of the urine hitting the water echoed in the small bathroom in his office. Finishing up, he flushed and turned the water on to wash his hands when the sound of gunshots ringing out. He immediately reached for his gun, only to realize he left it on the table out in the office.

"Fuck," he said to out loud just before clicking off the lights in the bathroom.

Dayvid sent two shots through the door and was in the office immediately before the two men counting money at the table could react. Dayvid hit the first one with a shot through his throat causing blood to spew from his mouth as he reached for his neck with both hands. The other men jumped back from the table knocking it over, sending some of the money flying up into the air as he lifted his gun letting off an errant shot. Dayvid squeezed his weapon with precision, landing three shots to the man's chest knocking him back over his chair.

Dayvid snatched the bag off his hip and quickly began scooping up the cash, even the ones with blood on them. He filled the bag and headed out the door into the hall, only to be met by gunshots coming from the far end of the hallway. Dayvid fired a few times at the big bodyguard looking niggas making them duck for cover, giving him enough time to make a dash for the back door and out into the alley just as the gunshots resumed flying at him. Dayvid ran as fast as he could down the shadowy alley as Pharaoh's crew spilled out the back door firing their guns at him. Barely able to see, Dayvid could hear the bullets hitting everything except him.

Suddenly he felt a pain in the side of his back causing him to stumble forward. "Arrgh!" he yelled putting his hand down to catch his balance from the force of being hit by a bullet. Dayvid regained his footing and made it to the end of the alley, quickly scaling the fence to the waiting Toyota Camry he had stolen and stashed days before for the getaway.

Pharaoh heard the shooting stop and slowly cracked open the door of bathroom. Just enough that he could press one eye up against it and see out. He watched as a man dressed in dark colored clothes stood over his two dead underlings and began scooping the money up into a bag. Pharaoh squinted trying to get a good look at the motherfucker brave enough to stick up his spot. As the man lifted up to leave, he was finally able to get a look at his face and couldn't believe his eyes. His mouth dropped open. Hell nah, he thought to himself. Pharaoh had just seen a ghost.

* * *

Dayvid slipped into his motel room undetected, the way he had most nights he went out on the prowl. He was in excruciating pain and had to take short breaths in order to get air into his lungs through all the discomfort. He tossed his gun and the bag of money onto one of the beds in the room and turned on the lamp on the nightstand. Slowly and gingerly removing his top layer of clothing he stripped down to the bullet proof vest he always sported and began unstrapping it. Barely able to lift his arms over his head, he was sore and suffering and struggled mightily to remove it. Dayvid looked in the mirror at the big, purplish bruise on the side of his ribs. From the way he couldn't take a deep breath, he assumed they might be broken. He gently walked over to the bed, hesitating before laying down, trying to prepare himself for a long sleepless night which was sure to be a painful one.

* * *

Pharaoh walked a few steps behind the thick, bronzed skinned stallion dressed only in a white spandex halter top and matching boy short panties, with a tattoo that covered her back and ran down the side of her leg. Her hips swayed as she walked and her ass bounced hypnotically causing him to fall under her spell as he admired the brick house of a woman. Pharaoh wondered what it would be like to fuck her and licked his lips with the thoughts of diving face first into that ass. She escorted him down the long entry way into the living room of the chic condo in the inner harbor.

On the couch with his feet up, in front of a large 72 inch flat screen built into the wall, dressed in a black wife beater and basketball shorts sat Saint. Enjoying a Thursday night football game between the Giants and Redskins, along with his partner Droop, a slim, light skinned dude who got his name from the shape of his sleepy eyes.

"You like football son?" Saint asked Pharaoh without turning to look at him.

"Yeah," he answered standing near the couch breathing heavily from the walk down the hallway.

"Who ya team, the Ravens?" Saint quizzed.

"Yeah," Pharaoh replied beaming with pride.

"Figures," he scoffed looking over at Droop who chuckled. Droop, like Saint, was originally from New York and though they didn't know each other back home, the roots they shared caused them to form a quick bond since being in Baltimore.

"Who winning?" Pharaoh asked as he moved to take a seat on the couch.

"Da fuck you doing my nigga?" Saint asked hitting mute on the TV. "Nigga you ain't got the luxury of sitting down to watch no fucking game. A lot of my bread is missing…on your watch, you need to be out in them streets handling that."

"That's what I came to holla at you about," Pharaoh said continuing to stand. "I know who it was that hit the club."

Saint sat up on the couch, Pharaoh had peaked his interest and now had his full attention. "Who nigga?" he inquired anxiously, his patience running thin.

"You gonna think I'm lunchin' but I swear it was King Dayvid," Pharaoh confessed.

"King Dayvid? Nigga is you smokin' dippers or something?" Saint asked. "You hear this shit, Droop? This nigga said King Dayvid."

Saint knew the name all too well. How could he ever forget? The nasty scar that stretched from his left shoulder and down across his chest was a daily reminder of his run-in with the infamous Porter family. About a year and a half ago, Saint came to Baltimore and set up shop with the help of OG Juan, a major player back in New York looking to expand his drug empire. He and a group of Juan's goons quickly carved out their own space in Baltimore's drug scene putting their murder game on display for anyone who opposed their regime. Saint, the most charismatic, became the de facto leader of the bunch, ascending to the top of the food chain and enjoying all the spoils of being the nigga on the throne. But the fact was, he was no more than a disposable figure head to a branch of Juan's empire. Something he would learn the hard way after falling hard for Fallon Porter. Through pillow talk she learned about the stash spot in a self-storage where he kept all the cash and bricks. The Porters wasted no time hitting it and clearing it out, leaving him holding the bag and in major debt to Juan. OG Juan feeling the need to make an example for others in his crew, summoned Saint back to New York. Upon his arrival he was beaten, tortured, shot and left for dead. Miraculously, he survived and fled to Virginia, where it didn't take the smooth talking New Yorker long to get back on his feet. Saint linked with a plug out in DC, then reached out to a few niggas that still fucked with him in B-More. Pharaoh being one of them and started moving weight again. He was the one fronting all the coke running through the strip club. Saint had put Pharaoh in a position to make more money than he ever had as a corner boy, gaining the round face hustler and his crew's loyalty. That relationship was allowing him to slowly ease back onto the scene of a city he had been run out of. Business was booming and Saint moved from Virginia back to Baltimore weeks earlier to keep a closer eye on his money.

"I'm serious," Pharaoh declared.

"Nigga you trying to be funny? Dayvid is dead," Saint proclaimed. "Rain is dead and that bitch Fallon is too, if I ever catch her," he spat venom in his words and rage in his eyes. He rose to his feet pulling the gun from under the pillow on his lap, cocking it and pressing the barrel of the gun to the middle of Pharaoh's forehead. "Nigga you dead too if you don't bring me my money or the head of the nigga who did it." Just the mention of one of the Porters had him seeing red. "Now get the fuck out my house."

Saint's glare was menacing as he watched the chubby hustler disappear out the living room before sitting back down on the couch to enjoy the rest of the game.

"Yo, what you wanna do wit that clown ass nigga?" Droop asked in his signature slow speech.

"Keep an eye on em. Any funny shit get rid of em," Saint replied coldly. "I hate fucking with these B-more niggas anyway."

9

"He who hates disguises it with his lips, but he lays up deceit in his heart. When he speaks graciously, do not believe him, for there are seven abominations in his heart." *-Proverb 26:24-25*

Nova was all smiles as she pranced around the great room in her new one bedroom loft apartment in the historic building on Tingey Street. It had only been a week since she moved in and she was still putting the finishing touches on her new place, making it feel like home. But the smile she wore was because of the guest she knew would be arriving at any moment. It had been forever since Nova had interest in anyone other than Dayvid. She had to think back to her earlier teenage years to remember the last person she was feeling that wasn't him. But the butterflies she felt knowing Saint was on the way and the warm tingle in her panties whenever she heard his voice on the phone, told her that she was definitely feeling Saint in a major way.

He was in town for the weekend, putting on a showcase for his new R&B artist they had spoken about on their first date. Instead of staying in a hotel Nova offered him to stay at her new place for the weekend. A bold step, but she liked the charismatic entrepreneur and wasn't one to front about her feelings or intentions.

Nova finally felt like herself again. Getting to know Saint and allowing herself to open up to a man other than Dayvid felt good. Saint got in town earlier that day but had been running around handling business. Nova had cooked while she waited for him to arrive. Her face lit up hearing the doorbell ring. Speed walking to the door, she placed her hand on the knob and took a deep breath before opening the door.

"What's up ma?" Saint said with a smile as he stood in the door. "Looking good like always," he flirted.

Nova blushed. "Come in," she said stepping to the side allowing him to pass.

"This is nice," he complimented looking around the loft apartment.

"Thank you," she replied. "I hope you worked up an appetite while you were running around all day. I cooked."

"Oh yeah?"

"Yes. Go put you bag in the room and come have a seat at the table while I fix your plate."

* * *

"Damn that was good," Saint complimented tossing his napkin down on to the empty plate. That's all a nigga want right there," he acknowledged.

"What's that?" Nova inquired.

"To make money, come home to good food and a woman he can trust," Saint explained.

"Is that right?" Nova replied liking what she heard.

The two of them had been spending every minute they could with one another when he was in town. Saint kept her smiling, something she thought she would never do again after losing Dayvid. Nova often wondered what Dayvid would have thought of the man sitting across from her. She hoped wherever he was in the afterlife he was smiling down on her and her new found interest. One thing Nova was sure about was that he would want her to definitely move on with her life and live. Dayvid was all she knew and now she was determined to try her hand at life and love again.

Nova didn't want to move too fast with Saint, she wanted to get to know him more in depth. However, she couldn't deny the chemistry and sexual attraction he and her shared. Saint was so sexy to Nova, from his good looks to the New York swag he possessed. He was bossed up and well put together. After being with Dayvid for so long it would have been almost impossible for Nova to be attracted to a blue collar, 9 to 5 ass nigga. Although she should have broadened her horizons in her choice of men after such a tragic loss, she liked only what she knows. Dayvid came along and saved her from her person hell. He loved her, molded her and took care of her that's all she knew. Dayvid was a King and she was his Queen. Deep down inside she yearned for the same caliber of a nigga.

The showcase was in a few hours and Nova wanted to look her best. She knew all types of people would be in attendance from: industry types, socialites and top hustling niggas, not to mention Saint's people. Nova hadn't met any of them yet, since Saint made sure all their time was spent with each other. Nova had showered right after they ate and was in her robe rummaging through her closet for something to wear. She had just done a little shopping a couple of days before but still couldn't decide on anything suitable for tonight's event. Nova was startled by the sound of Trey Songz "Jupiter Love" blaring from her living room. Nova exited her closet into the bedroom door just as Saint entered the room dressed in jeans and a wife beater.

He walked over wrapping his arms around her waist and began planting small kisses on her cheek.

Nova rubbed the scar on his shoulder and chest. "You ever gonna tell me how you got this?" she asked.

"It's a long story, something I really don't care to talk about," he explained.

Nova placed a soft kiss on his chest, then looked up at him. "I like it, it makes you unique."

"Yeah?" he laughed. "I never looked at it like that. What's wrong? I can see something is bothering you," he asked.

Nova walked back into the closet with a look of frustration on her face. "I have nothing to wear. Your party is in three hours and I have absolutely nothing to wear."

Saint smiled plopping down on the bed watching Nova sprout grey hairs stressing to find something. While she stood on her tip toes trying to reach for a box of shoes at the top of her closet, Saint admired the curves on her body. Nova's heart shaped bubble sat perfectly on her backside and her thick thighs enhanced her curves. Looking at Nova made his manhood rise and stiffen. He got up and walked behind her. Pulling her arms down and grabbing her waist. Saint leaned into her and spoke softly in her ear.

"All that shopping you did the other day and you can't find anything? How about you relax and let me pick something out for you to wear."

"Please," she laughed. "Move out my way wit your crazy self."

"No really," he said. "You can trust me. I got great taste. I chose you right?"

Nova leaned her head back on his shoulder and closed her eyes as she enjoyed his embrace and took in the smell of his Gucci cologne, not to mention the hard on pressing on her ass; Nova's kitty immediately began to throb. It had been quite some time since she felt the touch of a man or an erection pressed up against her. Saint had awakened the places that had laid dormant in her body and he could feel her body begging to be satisfied.

Saint gripped the side of her neck with his left hand, leaning it to the side as he licked and sucked it softly without leaving a love mark. His warm mouth and soft tongue made her nipples harden instantly. He used his other hand to palm her right breast, feeling the hardness of her nipple took his horniness to new heights. Groping and kissing Nova made his dick stretch a couple of more inches in his jeans. A soft moan escaped Nova's lips. At that moment all she was worried about went out the window. If they never made it anywhere that night it would have been alright with her as long as he could keep the feeling he was creating in her body going. Saint loosened the strings holding her robe together allowing it to fall to the floor, the sight of Nova's naked body caused Saint to grab his pole and bite down on his bottom lip. She was perfection and he wanted to feel her. The look in Nova's eyes showed him the feeling was mutual. Saint led her over to the bed, laid her on her back and proceeded to undress her. He stepped out of his jeans and underwear exposing his fully erect dick. Nova's eyes showed her approval of the girth of his love stick. Saint pulled her legs towards him, her sweet spot was clean shaven which impressed him. It made Nova even more inviting to him. Saint rubbed his dick against her clit in circular motions allowing her juices to flow freely. He then placed her legs on his shoulders and entered her. Nova was in pure bliss as Saint thrust in and out of her alternating speeds. The harder he

pumped, the louder her moans grew. Saint knew she was reaching her climax when he felt her legs lock and begin to tremble. Nova gyrated her hips and pumped her pussy in rhythm with him until she exploded on his dick. Nova was extremely turned on, her adrenaline was pumping and her love box was aching for more. She jumped up, pushed Saint onto the bed and straddled him. His thickness caused her to hold her breath upon his entry, but her wetness made it easy to glide up and down on his pole, bringing her to a fast, but steady rhythm. Saint gripped her ass cheeks while he enjoyed the tightness of her sweet spot. Nova grinded and clenched her pussy muscles while she creamed all over his dick. Saint turned her over on all fours and entered her from behind and began pounding her into submission. Saint was getting closer to his climax with every moan Nova made. The louder she got, the harder he went, and the wetter she became. It wasn't long before he let out a pleasurable groan as he spilled his seed on Nova's backside.

Nova laid on her stomach, exhausted and breathing heavy. Every part of her body was sensitive down to her fingertips. Saint leaned over and kissed the nape of her neck followed by a trail of small ones down her back before standing up and walking into the closet. After a few seconds, he re-emerged holding a dress in his hand.

"I think you'll kill em in this," smiling as he laid it on the bed next to her. "Either way you'll be the baddest woman in the room," he said continuing to smile before proceeding to the bathroom and turning on the shower.

Nova sat up on her elbows, admiring the man who had just put her body through a workout. She smiled and shook her head. "This muthafucka here."

* * *

The club filled quickly, exactly what Saint had hoped for when he linked up with one of the best promoters in DC. Bar 7, a sultry, upscale lounge located in the heart of downtown proved to be the perfect place for the artist showcase and label launch party. The state of the art sound system pumped out the latest hits, while the record company's logo projected on the walls of the luxurious spot in lights. Waitresses carried bottles of Ciroc, accompanied by sparklers to various tables throughout the venue, while people mixed and mingled enjoying the ambiance. Saint soaked it all in from the VIP area amongst record execs, radio program directors, magazine editors and big name music producers, all in attendance to see what he had to offer to the music game. He moved around the VIP, in and out of conversations with different people, all while keeping one eye glued to the front door, anticipating Nova's arrival. He kept replaying their sexual encounter from earlier that night and although he was there to handle business, he couldn't get her off his mind; how soft she felt, her intoxicating scent. The thought of how she taste made him lick his lips hoping her juices would still be there. To a nigga like Saint, women were an accessory that he wore for a night or two before it was time to switch up. Nova was different from the women he was used to. She was independent, didn't hound or stress him and didn't need him to take care of her, which ironically made him want to.

Droop bopped over to Saint and stood next to him. "Damn, nigga!" he said handing him a drink. "This some fly shit you put together."

"Yeah, you know how I do," Saint bragged. "But yo, why you bring sand to the beach?" Saint inquired looking over his shoulder at the woman sitting at a table filled with food and bottles.

"Nigga that's my baby moms," Droop shook his head. "Trust me, I would have never heard the end of it if I ain't bring that bitch. It's cool tho, putting her ass to work," he laughed.

"Whatchu mean?"

"I put the bricks in her trunk. She's driving the shit back and don't even know it." Droop revealed.

Saint just shook his head and smiled.

His smile grew wider when he saw Nova walk through the door dressed in a white bodycon dress and orange Olcay Gulsen ankle strap pumps. Her beauty was undeniable and her dressed hugged every curve of her frame perfectly, showing off her thick thighs, hips and ass. Nova's strut was regal, moving as though she knew she had the crown jewel between her legs. Saint watched as heads turned trying to get a look at her as she made her way through the crowd. Every nigga in the room was trying to get her attention, they would love to be the lucky one who went home with her. Saint poked his chest out slightly, feeling like a king knowing people were admiring the woman who came to the party with eyes only for him.

"You see that my nigga?" Droop asked when his eyes landed on the shapely beauty heading for to the bar.

"Yeah, that's Renee," Saint beamed with pride.

"That's shorty?" Droop asked in admiration. "Nice," he said in his signature slow, laid back tone.

"I'll be right back," he said as he slid away to go greet her. Saint cut through the crowd hastily, easing up behind Nova at the bar and whispering in her ear. "You know you the baddest thing in here, right?"

Nova blushed enjoying the compliment. "Am I?" she asked rhetorically.

Saint wrapped his arms around her waist. Pulling her into him and enjoying the feeling of her soft, plumped ass rubbing against his dick, he kissed her on the cheek. "Yes," he answered even though he knew she knew it.

She felt his dick beginning to swell in his pants and wiggled up against him teasing it. She liked being wanted and Saint made her feel like the sexiest woman on the planet when he was around. "I don't have on any panties," she confessed.

"You not playing fair," he said fighting the urge to leave but knowing he needed to handle his business. "Come on, I got a table back there," he motioned for her to accompany him to the VIP section.

Droop kept his eyes on Saint and Nova as they talked by the bar. Saint wasn't the type of nigga to move with a bodyguard but Droop would be the closest thing to it if he had one. Saint kept him close, he respected Droop's gangster and knew he was respected in the streets. He saw Droop as an ally in a foreign land. But Droop didn't necessarily see things the same way, he didn't give a fuck about the two of them being from New York. His only concern was making as much money as possible. That's why he played Saint so close, he was hoping to get introduced to the plug from DC. He made it his business to come to the party, thinking the source of the bricks Saint was getting his hands on would show up. Droop had plans on being the man, something he hid well behind his sleepy look. He would kill for that crown and once Saint plugged him in, he was a dead man.

Droop's concentration was interrupted by the manicured hand of his baby mother rubbing across the back of his neck. "What you staring at nigga? Don't get slapped in here," she said jokingly.

Tajha, was a slim and curvy redbone, who worked as a dancer at Norma Jean's. She was bad in her on right with slanted, hazel eyes, full lips, a long black weave with a Chinese bang and an even longer list of ballers she fucked. She was originally from Baltimore and shared a 2-year-old son with Droop, something he regretted every day. Their relationship was rocky at best, always on and off again.

"What da fuck you talkin' bout?" he said slightly annoyed, immediately wishing he hadn't brought her along.

"I see you watching that bitch, just like every other nigga in here," Tajha said.

"Shut the fuck up, Taj. You drawin. That's my nigga Saint girl," he informed her.

"Oh really, she done hooked another one huh," she sneered.

"Whatchu mean hooked another one?" he inquired interested in any information about the female speaking with Saint.

"You don't know who that is?" she asked astonished by his ignorance.

"Nah," he squinted his eyes trying to see if he had missed something.

"That's Nova. She was King Dayvid's girl."

"See there you go Taj, talkin' shit you don't know. Shorty name Renee," Droop stated frowning up his face at how far off base she was.

"No the hell it ain't! That's Nova," she spoke up more boisterous, sure of her accurate recollection.

"How you so sure?" Droop asked seeing her passionate reaction.

"Nigga! Every bitch and they mama wanted King Dayvid, me included," she added. "And every bitch knew the bitch who had em. No matter how low key he tried to keep her, females talk. He moved her out to Owings Mills or Cockeysville or something like that, but that's definitely her."

Droop just nodded his head and stored the tidbit of info his baby mother had just supplied him with. The two of them stopped talking as they saw Saint and his lady friend walking towards them.

Saint could feel the envious eyes on him as he walked hand in hand leading Nova through VIP and he loved it. "Renee this my manz, Droop and his wifey Taj," he said reaching their table.

"Nice to meet you both," Nova said forcing a smile. She wasn't a fan of meeting new people, something that had rubbed off on her from years of dealing with Dayvid.

"What's up," Droop replied.

"Nice to meet you too," Taj said. "Girl I love them shoes!"

"Thank you," Nova said. She definitely didn't fuck with new bitches. She found them extremely nosey, catty and jealous but she decided to play nice out of respect for Saint and his event.

The evening was going well, Nova had begun to warm up to Droop and Taj and she was actually having a great time. Saint looked so good to her standing on the stage introducing his artist. She found herself staring at him, thinking about what it would be like to be his woman. He was the total opposite of what she was used to and she had to admit to herself that she really was enjoying the change. No one could ever replace Dayvid in her heart. The things she knew about life and love, she had learned either with him or from him. The love she had for him was one of a kind, something that could never be duplicated. But Nova's heart had begun the healing process and she was ready take a chance with Saint.

Smiling from ear to ear as he walked towards her, she kissed him on his cheek when he reached her. Only to have him grab her and pull her into his chest and kiss her on the lips. They stood nodding their heads along with everybody in attendance at the young female singer on the stage killing her performance.

Nova leaned over to Saint and whispered," I need to go to the bathroom. Where is it?"

"Come on, I'll walk with you," he said.

Nova laughed. "I'll be ok Saint. I can go by myself. Where is it?"

"It's over there," he pointed then watched her until she disappeared into the crowd.

Droop approached, tapping Saint on the shoulder. "Yo we bout to hit this highway, head back to B-More."

Saint gave him a pound and a half hug." Thanks for coming through my nigga."

"No doubt, it's all G. A lil' business, a lil' pleasure that's always a good thing," Droop proclaimed. "But check this out my nigga, I got some information you might be interested in."

"What's that?"

"Shorty you fucking with, ain't keeping it a hunnit wit' you. I don't know what she hiding but she ain't who you think she is," Droop kicked it, his sleepy eyes lower than normal from all the liquor in his system.

"Fuck you talkin' bout?" Saint said turning to face him. The look on his face said he was looking for nothing less than a straight answer. The new woman in his life was definitely something of a mystery and he wanted to know what Droop knew.

"First off her name ain't Renee," he started. "Her name is Nova and she was King Dayvid's main bitch."

"Word," Saint said surprised by the news. But wanting to know more. "You sure about that?"

"100 percent. I got it on a real reliable source," he assured.

Saint had a puzzled look on his face but he also had no reason to question what Droop was telling him. "Good looking my nigga," he said dapping up Droop again.

"Yeah, you know you can't trust these bitches," he said looking directly in Taj's direction before signaling to her it was time to go.

Droop's words played in Saint's head as he stood alone sipping a drink in his hand. "You definitely can't trust these bitches," he mumbled to himself. "I wonder what else she's hiding?" he pondered. All the questions he had immediately began to make sense. How she had been able to afford staying in that hotel for so long, her fly condo, the shopping sprees. Dayvid must've left her straight, he thought to himself. This bitch probably sitting on a couple million or something. This nigga was hitting banks, jewelry stores, all type of shit. I know he had a stash. He rubbed his hands together, all his vices- avarice and perfidy bubbling to the surface. The Porters had taken from him and now he was going to take pleasure in returning the favor. It was obvious that Nova didn't know who he was or his history with the Porters. She also was feeling him, something else he planned on using to in his advantage. *All I gotta do is keep fucking this bitch good and she gonna lead a nigga right to that paper,* he thought to himself. He hated the Porters with a passion. Now he was fucking King Dayvid's girl and was about to get his hands on all his paper. As he looked up, seeing Nova strutting back across the room, he no longer saw the beautiful woman he was trying to court and impress. All he could think about looking in her face was revenge and like the old saying went; it was a dish best served cold.

10

"When the wicked, even mine enemies and my foes, came upon me to eat up my flesh, the stumbled and fell." *-Psalm 27:2*

U.S. Marshal Palmeri twisted the top off the bottle of Excedrin and turned it up to his mouth then downed the warm mug of coffee on his desk. He watched as his partner stood in a trance, mumbling incoherently in front of a board with photos on it. He had grown tired of Torrence's obsession with the case, a case which he felt had basically closed itself. Fallon and Autumn were now both in Mexico, out of their jurisdiction and Dayvid and Rain were dead. But Torrence refused to let it go.

"You don't find it funny that this woman here," she said pointing at a picture of a beautiful brown skinned woman carrying shopping bags. "Renee Preston, seemed to appear out of nowhere. Looking at the records, it's like she didn't even exist until a few years ago. And now she pops up spending a shit load of marked money from a heist, that it is common knowledge the Porters did," Torrence said turning to face her partner.

"I just don't think it's worth pursuing. Half the Porters are dead, and the other half are out of the country. I don't think this woman is of any importance," Palmeri explained.

"Do you know the Porters' lawyer was found dead in his apartment, only hours after it was reported Dayvid was dead?"

"And?" Palmeri asked. "Morganstein was as crooked as they came. He was in bed with all type of shady characters including the Russian mob, no telling who killed him."

"Maybe she killed him as a way to clean up some of the Porters loose ends," Torrence suggested.

"Really?" Palmeri shook his head at her far-fetched assumption.

"You never know. Why is she hiding out in a hotel?"

"And what about that guy, where does he fit into all this?" Palmeri asked pointing at a picture of Saint.

"That's Charles St. Clair, or Saint. He is a mid-level drug dealer who is slowly on the rise out in Baltimore. His name came up in a case in New York from a few years ago. He worked for a major player in the drug game. That is until he was robbed for a large shipment out in Baltimore by guess who?" she asked.

"The Porters."

"Yes," she yelled. "Now when he got back to New York, this major player was not happy and attempted to kill Saint but luckily he survived."

"So he has an axe to grind with the Porters," Palmeri said as the wheels in his mind began turning. "I wonder if we let him know that this woman is somehow connected to the Porters would he be willing to assist us in connecting the dots."

"Now you're thinking," she said.

* * *

Droop unlocked the door to Taj's apartment and stepped inside. His hands were filled with bags from his latest trip to the mall. He had purchased a bunch of clothes and sneakers for his son and wanted to surprise him with it. In a good mood, he had even copped something for her. He called her name a few times but after receiving no answer, he put the bags down and headed to the kitchen. Clicking on the light, he was startled by the presence of an unexpected visitor sitting at the kitchen table with his sleeping son on his lap and his baby mother tied up in the chair next to him with tape over her mouth.

"Dayvid!" Droop said in fright. "What the fuck are you doing here?" he asked, seeing the same timorous look in Taj's eyes as if she wanted to know the same time.

"Heard you the man now," Dayvid said as he stared coldly at Droop while continuing to bounce the sleeping little boy on his lap.

"Nah G, you heard wrong," he stated trying to sound convincing.

"Let's not make this get any uglier than it has to. But if you lie to me again, the sound of me blowing your baby moms head off is gonna wake your son up," he promised then raised his gun sitting it on the table in front of him.

Droop stared in his eyes trying to find any inkling of apprehension but found none. He knew Dayvid meant every word. His focus immediately shifted to staying alive and keeping his family that way as well. But he knew the fact that Dayvid wasn't masked up didn't bode well for their chances of survival.

"I got bread but it ain't here," Droop said as Dayvid sat silent staring at him. "Not the type of bread I know you looking for," Droop continued.

Dayvid lifted the gun off the table and put it to Taj's head. She tried to scream but the tape over her mouth wouldn't let her. She was only able to manage a muffled cry as tears started running down her face.

"I'm telling you the truth, I swear," Droop begged. "I don't live here, this is not my crib. Me and her are not together like that. I promise you."

Taj's began shaking her head in agreement while continuing to pray and cry.

"I could give you all my little bit of bread fam and you probably still gonna kill me and my baby moms," Droop expressed. "Or I can put you on to a nigga with a lot more money than me and give you something I'm sure is worth more than money to you."

"Ain't nothing worth more than money to me right now, so stop stalling before I put your son in the blender and make you sip him through a straw," Dayvid barked.

"Not even Nova?" Droop asked.

"Whatchu say?"

"I said is Nova worth more than money to you?"

Just hearing her name made Dayvid's heart begin to race in his chest. His palms dampened and beads of sweat formed on his brow. He moved his gun off of Taj and pointed at Droop again. "What you know about Nova?" he asked.

"Promise me you'll let us live and I'll tell you," Droop bargained.

"I ain't making no promises, cuz you gonna tell me either way. You not really in the position to be making demands."

Droop assessed the situation and agreed with him. "I know where she is," he stated. "She's in DC. She's fucking with my connect, a nigga named Saint. He's getting it. He got a spot out here in the harbor but he be back and forth. You can kill two birds with one stone, get your girl and his money," Droop purposed.

"Yeah I know Saint, but ain't no way Nova fucking with a nigga like that," Dayvid proclaimed.

"I swear on my son. Ask her," he said pointing to Taj. "We just was with them at a party in DC."

"You scream you die," Dayvid informed her before snatching the tape off her mouth.

Taj let out a slight whimper from the sting of the tape being pulled off. "He is telling the truth. We were just with them both in DC at Bar 7. Please, he is telling you the truth. Don't hurt my son please," she begged.

"I ain't gonna hurt your son, Slim," he said to her. "But I will take that little bit of bread you said you had here," Dayvid told Droop. "And those house keys, just in case I gotta come back here if y'all not telling the truth. Oh, and let me get your cell phone," Dayvid said to Taj.

* * *

"Oh my God," Nova shouted as she collapsed onto Saint's chest trying to catch her breath after another pleasure filled sex session. The two had been locked in the house for 3 days going at it like a bunch of teenagers, only breaking to eat and sleep. Saint's latest weekend visit had turned into a week-long one and Nova was enjoying every moment, especially having a warm body to lay next to at night. She liked having Saint around and wished he would stay full time, a fact she contemplated mentioning to him but hadn't yet. She wasn't exactly sure if she wanted him to move in or just move to DC, either way she wanted more of his time.

Saint ran his fingers through her hair as she laid on his chest, he too had felt her growing closer to him and could tell that she was looking to make more of their relationship. She was playing right into his hands and he continued to reel her in every chance he gets.

"What you thinking about?" Nova asked looking up at him staring at the ceiling.

"How these moments are too fleeting," he said tugging at the emotions he knew she felt.

"I was thinking the same thing," she said feeling a sense of relief that he was feeling similar to her and that he had said it first.

"I'm thinking about being in DC a little more, maybe permanently. I have a lot of things going on out here with my artist being here and my…" he let his voice tail off purposely.

"Your what?" Nova asked wanting to know how he viewed her status in his life.

"You know… you, my lady," Saint said sounding like music to her ears.

"Your lady? So you just claiming shit as your own now," she teased.

"You not mine? It's not mine?" he asked sliding his hand between her legs and slipping his fingers in her still wet crevice.

Nova moaned softly and kissed his bottom lip. She was ready to go another round.

Saint relished in her quivering for his touch. *I got this bitch right where I want her,* he thought to himself, only to be interrupted by his phone ringing. Saint ignored it the first time but after it began ringing again, Nova told him to answer it as she jumped up from the bed.

"I'm gonna go make us something to eat," she said before walking her thick naked body out the room.

Saint looked at his phone, seeing the familiar number on the screen he quickly answered. "Yo Droop, what up?" he said into the phone only to be taken aback by the voice on the other end of the phone.

"No Saint, this is Taj."

Saint sat up on the side of the bed. "The fuck you doing calling me from this nigga's phone Taj? You trying to get us caught?" he asked. "What the fuck is you thinking?"

"This ain't that type of call baby," she spoke softly into the phone. "You ain't gonna be so worried about this nigga when I tell you how much of a snake he is," she vented.

"What you talking bout?" Saint said standing to his feet and walking over to the window.

"This nigga Dayvid had me in here tied up and shit, holding my son Tyreke in his arms and all that. This nigga Droop walked in and panicked. He started giving you up to save his own ass."

"What? Dayvid who?" a confused Saint asked.

"King Dayvid," she confessed.

"Hold up, slow down," he told her. "King Dayvid is still alive?" he asked. *Damn that nigga Pharaoh wasn't lying,* he thought.

"Yes, and he had a gun to my head," she started to cry thinking about how close she came to dying. "And my son's head threatening to kill him," she amped it. "And this bitch ass nigga Droop ain't do shit. Just gave him you, told him all about you and his girl, Nova."

Saint immediately knew it was true, Taj was nowhere around when the two of them discussed Renee being Nova. *This fucking nigga is alive,* he thought to himself. *And this python ass nigga Droop sent him at me,* his mind was racing. "I'm gonna call you back, keep your phone close."

"That's the thing, he took my phone," Taj revealed as Saint banged on her.

Saint rubbed both his hands over his head and down across his face, exhaling a deep breath. A giant sized monkey wrench was just thrown into his plan and he needed to think fast as to what he was gonna do.

He was brought from his deep thought by the delicious smell of steak and eggs entering the room. Nova stood in front of him naked holding a plate in one hand and a glass of juice and the other.

"Damn ma, you make a nigga never want to leave," Saint said looking her up and down, her body was amazing. "That food look good, I'm bout to tear that shit up. I'm starving,"

"You just make sure you save some room for me," she flirted shifting her hips back and forth before handing him his plate.

"Oh, you know I got you," he smiled.

* * *

May 2014

"Look at the car swerving back and forth," Rain joked as she blew out a cloud of weed smoke. "Fallon bout to make that nigga crash."

"Chill slim, nobody wanna hear that shit," Dayvid growled taking the weed out of her hand and hitting it. He didn't want to think about what his sister might be doing in the truck a few car lengths in front of them. He was more concern about the nigga with her or more importantly his drug stash and where he kept it.

Fallon was riding with Saint, a hustler from New York, who had recently set up shop in Baltimore and was moving heavy weight along with his out of town crew. Every chick in the city wanted to be the first one to cuff the new money getting nigga with the New York plates. It was like a badge of honor amongst the sack chasers. Fallon had more game than most, she brought Saint to her, acting uninterested which only made him pursue her harder. All part of the plan that Dayvid and Rain had put together, Saint was marked from the jump.

"Call Autumn," Dayvid said.

Rain dialed and waited for her baby sister to pick up, then passed the phone to him.

"Hello," Autumn answered.

"We ready, make it happen," he instructed.

"Ok."

Autumn hung up and stood up off the bed, the whole time

keeping her gun trained on the bounded and gagged man in a chair in the middle of the motel room. She calmly approached him and place her gun to the side of his head. "It's showtime," she said. "Remember we know where ya mother, ya grandmother and ya baby mother stay," she threatened as she removed his gag. Autumn picked the man's phone up, dialed a number and place it to his ear.

Saint moaned lightly as Fallon used her mouth to please him. The more he squirmed the harder she went, taking him deeper into her mouth until he could feel the back of her throat. Fallon was a super freak and he loved it. Saint's phone beginning to light up and buzz didn't stop her, Fallon never broke her up and down motion as he reached to answer his phone.

"Yo," he said.

"Yo what up Saint, this Run from the Westside," the voice on the other end of the phone said.

"What's good my nigga?"

"Same shit, different toilet, I can't call it. But it's that time, I need to see you," Run said letting him know he needed to re-up.

"Whatchu talkin?" Saint asked.

"The usual," Run informed him.

"Bet, I'll be at you in a few," Saint said hanging up the phone.

"Yo, I gotta make a stop real quick," Saint told Fallon as she stopped and sat up in her seat. "Then I promise, no more interruption the rest of the night, just me and you," he charmed.

"Yeah, whatever," Fallon pouted, pretending to be upset.

Dayvid made sure to stay a few cars back and not to follow the black truck to close. He didn't want to risk fucking up the lick but more importantly he didn't want to put his sister in anymore danger than she already was. He knew Fallon could handler herself but the quicker this was over the better. Seeing the truck's blinker come on and the vehicle switch lanes, Dayvid followed suit and merged onto the highway behind them.

Exiting the highway Dayvid had an intense look on his face watching Saint's truck pull into a U-haul self-storage and stop at the gate.

"C'mon Fallon, don't fuck this up," he voiced his concern.

"She got it," Rain reassured him as they watched Saint's reach his arm out the window and dial in the code.

"7498#," Fallon memorized to herself, watching out the corner of her eye while pretending to be on Twitter. She typed it into her phone and pressed send as they drove through the gate.

Saint stopped the truck in front of building 39 and cut off the engine. "I'll be right back," he said reaching in the backseat retrieving a blue duffle bag.

Dayvid looked down at his phone and back up as he punched in the gate code then cut his lights off as he entered the property. Slowly navigated the storage place, he turned the corner and spotted Saint's truck. Dayvid threw it in park, cut off the engine and him and Rain quickly jumped out with their guns in hand.

Saint stepped out the storage unit and began lowering the door when he heard the familiar sound of guns being cocked. He immediately knew what was happening. "Fuck," he whispered to himself.

"Don't close up shop just yet slim," Dayvid instructed.

Saint turned to see himself surrounded by all three Porters with guns drawn. He stared at Fallon with hatred burning in his eyes wanting to put a bullet right between her eyes. "You fucking grimy bitch," he mumbled, only to feel Dayvid's gun hit him in the face opening up a large gash under his eye. "Arrgh."

"Who the fuck you calling a bitch, bitch nigga," Dayvid barked as he grabbed him and forced his gun into his mouth. "Say that shit again!"

"Chill D, let's get what we came for and get the fuck outta here, fuck this nigga," Rain said as she placed her hand on his shoulder trying to calm him down and refocus him. "Fallon go pull the car around," she yelled.

Rain lifted the door and Dayvid push a bloodied Saint back into the storage unit. The two siblings were taken aback at the amount of bricks of coke inside, they were stacked up almost to the ceiling looking like a white wall. They had underestimated Saint, he was holding enough cocaine to flood the city a few times over.

"Gotdamn," Rain blurted out saying what they both was thinking.

"Get on your knees and put your hands behind ya back," Dayvid instructed Saint pressing his gun to the back of his head.

Saint did as he was told as Rain quickly used zip ties on his hands and feet to subdue him. The Porters then proceed to empty the entire unit out.

When they were done Dayvid walked over to Saint, who was laid out on the floor and pointed his gun down at him. "Consider this a warning, get out of Baltimore. If I see you again, I'ma put a bullet in your head," then he turned and exited the empty unit leaving Saint inside. "Don't worry somebody should be here in the morning to let you out," he said as he lowered the door and pad locked it.

Saint watched as the room went dark.

* * *

Saint rolled over and stretched his body trying to work the soreness from his legs. Sex with Nova was like a workout. Her sex drive was unmatched by any woman he had ever been with before. *I see why this nigga kept this bitch around,* he said to himself, thinking about their last session that was responsible for the sleep coma he had just awaken from. Saint pulled the covers off of him and sat on the side of the bed. The glimmer of light from the streetlights outside escaped through the blinds allowing him to see inside the dark room. Saint looked back over his shoulder at the woman sleeping in the bed next to him. For a brief moment he allowed himself to feel for her. Truth was she was a good woman, any man would be proud to call her his. But she was mixed up in something that was bigger than her, his vendetta was much stronger than his feelings for her and

although he knew she was innocent in the war between him and the Porters, he didn't care. Saint was tired of playing. Knowing Dayvid was alive and looking from him and Nova meant he was on the clock. He picked his jeans off the floor on the side of the bed, slid them on and stood up. Opening the top drawer of the nightstand, he grabbed his gun.

"Nova get up," he ordered pointing the gun at her sleep on the bed. "Get the fuck up, you're coming with me," he repeated pulling the covers off of her. "What the fuck!" he said in shock looking down at the pillows laying on the bed in her place. "Damn, you can't trust these bitches!" he said through clenched teeth upset with himself. He clicked on the lights and began searching the apartment but she was nowhere to be found, Nova was in the wind. "She must've heard me on the phone," he spoke out loud, seeing every trace of her gone. Saint walked into Nova's closet which was a mess with things tossed everywhere. He noticed that the rug had been lifted up in the back of the closet at the base of the wall. Peeling the rug back he saw the empty safe in the floor. "Fuck!" he screamed banging his hands on top of his head, holding his gun is his right hand. "The fucking money been right here the whole time," he said kicking a hole in the wall. Saint pulled out his phone and dialed a number. "Yo, I need you to do something for me," he barked while exiting the closet in haste, snatching his shirt and keys before storming out the apartment.

11

"Now there was long war between the house of Saul and house of David: But David waxed stronger and stronger, and the house of Saul waxed weaker and weaker." *-2 Samuel 3:1*

The signs passed like blurry streaks of green as Nova raced up I-95 towards Baltimore, her heart rate matching the speedometer. The pounding in her chest made it feel like her heart would leap through her shirt at any moment. Going off of fear and adrenaline, Nova gave no thought to the highway patrol as she zoomed through traffic; constantly checking her rearview to see if she had been followed. *Who else knows? No telling whose been watching me.* The thought frightened her and the black duffle bag full of money in her trunk had her nerves fried. She knew niggas wouldn't hesitate to kill for that type of come up and she was an easy target. All that ran through her mind while trying to process the conversation she overheard Saint having on the phone.

"He's alive?" she shouted in disbelief almost unable to accept it as truth. *How is he alive? Why would he let me think he was dead?* she thought, her eyes flamed with hatred.

It had taken everything in Nova to remain even keel and consistent throughout the night, trying not to tip her hand or set off any alarms in Saint. Just hearing Dayvid's name threw her out of whack mentally and she struggled all night to keep her focus. Continuing her sex filled weekend with Saint became extremely difficult, the mixture of emotions almost was too much to bear. Nova thought back to the many nights she had to check out mentally and numb herself in order to deal with the sexual abuse she suffered at the hands of Redd. That allowed her to feel nothing as she put on a performance that put Saint into a deep slumber. Once she was sure he was out cold, she moved quickly, putting her plan in motion. She fought back tears gathering her things not wanting to second guess herself. She had been through so much finding the strength to begin anew but her and Dayvid's hearts were like magnets and she would go to the ends of the earth to find him. The revelation of his resurrection was somewhat bittersweet though, she had allowed herself to dream again, to feel, to open up to the chance of being loved again. It was now Saint she visualized when she thought about her future. But to hear him on the phone with another woman, speaking about her true identity and mentioning Dayvid, fear overtook her and made Nova question his intentions, making the decision to flee an easy one. She had let her guards down and unknowingly let an enemy in her gates. "How could I be so stupid," she yelled. "I should've known better."

Nova knew Dayvid better than anyone and figured that if he was back in Baltimore, willing to risk all the effort he had put forth in convincing the world of his demise, he had good reason. "Or least he better had," she thought out loud. As she entered the city limits, Nova prayed that she was the reason. The money in her trunk was more than enough for them to start a new life in Mexico like they had planned. But finding him would be a problem, Dayvid had mastered the ability to move in the shadows when needed. She tried to get inside his head and think like him. *Where are you Dayvid?* she racked her brain. Finally, it hit her, Nova flicked on her turn signal and exiting the highway.

The sun had just begun to creep across the morning sky when she pulled on the block, parking in front of the United Methodist Church on the corner. Nova took a series of deep breaths trying to reel in her jittery nerves. Looking at her reflection in the rearview mirror she saw red, puffy eyes staring back at her. She began wiping away the tears, preparing to come face to face with the man she'd spent the last decade of her life loving. She didn't know exactly how to feel, what she would say or how she who react; it had been months since she laid eyes on Dayvid. *Did he move on with his life? Why the fuck didn't he try to find me? Maybe that letter about me moving on was all bullshit, just a way for him to move on with his life. So you fake your fucking death?* Her mind was overloaded with questions. Nova didn't know what she would see or who for that matter when she knocked on the door of the hideout. *If there's a bitch in here I'ma kill him myself.* She wasn't certain he would even be there but it was worth a try. The apartment wasn't in the prettiest of neighborhoods, but Nova knew if shit got hot this was one of the many places he might go. She scanned the block, searching for the old Acura he used when he wanted to keep a low profile but it was nowhere in sight. Popping open the glove box to retrieve the gun she had hidden inside, Nova cut off the engine and exited the car. "Bitch, get yourself together, your fucking man is alive. Fuck all the questions, save that shit for later," she gave herself a quick pep talk before she walked in on something that would change her life again. Her hands shook nervously, feeling as though she would choke from the anxiety but she was determine not to let it defeat her. Nova was on a mission to find Dayvid. She knew in her heart that no matter what he was going through or who he was with, she was what he needed.

Keeping a firm grip on the handgun in her handbag, Nova powerwalked up the block until she reached the rundown home. Her heartbeat quickened with every step. Nova pulled the gun from her bag as she walked to the back of the home, prepared for anything. Reaching the door she knocked a few times. The seconds seemed

like hours as she stood there waiting for it to open. After knocking a few more times Nova began looking around to see if she could find where he might have hidden a key. Kicking the trash and leaves on the ground, hoping something would jump out or look out of place.

Come on Nova, think. She looked down at the slab of concrete wedged against the side of the house and crouched down trying to move it. After a few tries she was able to lift it up and saw the key peeking out of the dirt underneath.

She slid the key in, unlocking the door and slowly pushed it open. "Hello," she said proceeding with caution into the dark apartment. Feeling along the wall she located the light and clicked it on. She could feel his presence, almost like a ghostly spirit and knew he had been there. As she walked deeper in the basement apartment the remnants of him were everywhere. A pair of pants and a shirt hanging on the back of the couch and a half empty 2-liter Root Beer sitting out on the counter let Nova know for sure that he had been there. She picked the shirt up off the couch and smelled it, inhaling his scent. Tears began to form in her eyes again as all the memories they shared played in her head like a flipagram clip. Though he had been there it was obvious that he wasn't coming back. She was so close but yet still so far away. Feeling overwhelmed she exited the apartment not bothering to close the door behind her.

"This wasn't supposed to be like this," Nova spoke through tears as she rode around aimlessly trying to figure out her next move.

"We're supposed to be in Mexico, living happily ever after and shit." All out of ideas and exhausted Nova decided to head to Towson. The rent on the condo was paid up for a year, she figured she could get some rest and stash the loot. Riding around with all that money wasn't smart. A soft dinging sound broke her train of thought. Nova looked at the dashboard, the orange fuel light was blinking. "Damn!" There was no way she was making it to Baltimore County without stopping for gas. Nova spotted a Shell gas station a block away and switched lanes.

Nova turned her Cadillac ATS into the gas station parking lot on South Caton Avenue and pulled up to the pump. She jumped out, hit the alarm and hurried inside. Entering the store, she headed straight to the back to grab a bottle of water.

"Will that be all ma'am?" the man behind the counter asked smiling at the beautiful woman standing in front of him.

"Can I get 25 on 2," Nova answered casually.

The music was blasting as Jaz whipped the Yukon Denali into the gas station parking lot pulling into one of the parking spots in front of the store. "Yo, get a box of swishers," he instructed his homie exiting the on the passenger side. "Strawberry nigga!" he yelled turning down the music and rolling down his window. Jaz adjusted his posture in the seat to get a better look at the bad bitch with the plump ass strolling out the store as his man held the door open for her.

"What up ma, you looking good," he complimented. "Come

fuck with a real nigga," he offered.

Uninterested in his advances, Nova kept it moving straight to her vehicle. *That young nigga can't be serious*, she thought to herself about the baby face hustler continuing her trek to the pump.

Jaz kept his eyes glued to her ass through the rearview following it all the way to her vehicle. "That bitch got ass for days," he said to the nigga in the backseat breaking up some weed.

Nova yawned, leaning up against the car waiting for her tank to fill up. The rush of excitement had begun to wear off and she was exhausted. The comfortable bed at her condo was calling her name and she couldn't wait to snuggle under the covers. Nova stared angrily at the gas pump total rise, wishing it would move faster, she was ready to go.

"Yo ma, you out here pumping your own gas?" Jaz shouted out the window.

Nova hadn't noticed him pull up on the side of her.

"See I told you, you need to fuck wit' a real nigga. I would've took care of that for you."

Nova, growing tired of his attempts to spark a conversation, turned her back to him and waited for her gas to finish.

"Damn, how you gonna act like that," he continued.

Before Nova could answer the back door of the truck flew open. Pharaoh and the dude who held the door open for her hopped out waving guns. Nova screamed but Pharaoh grabbed her by the neck, shoving his gun in her face. Nova's eyes grew wide and round as dinner plates.

"Grab her keys," he ordered the other man with the gun.

Pharaoh pushed Nova forcefully into the backseat of the truck. "Shut the fuck up bitch," he yelled hitting her in the back of the head with the butt of his gun as she screamed trying to draw attention. Nova instantly became disorientated and dizzy, reaching for the back of her head she felt the wet warmth of blood on her hand. Pharaoh jumped in next to her and Jaz slammed down on the gas pulling out of the parking lot as the other member of their crew followed in Nova's car.

* * *

"Meet me at the spot on North Ave," Saint barked instruction into the phone.

He hung up and immediately scrolled through his contacts until he reached Taj's number. Dayvid had her phone and he figured it was worth a shot to see if he would answer. Saint pressed send and listened as the phone rang once… twice…and a third times before it picked up on the other end. There was a deafening silence as the two men waited to see who would be the first to speak. Almost thirty seconds passed before Saint broke the dead air. "Dayvid Porter, it's been a minute."

Still he received no response but the faint sound of Dayvid's breathing, letting him know he was listening. "I'm gonna keep this short and sweet. I got something I know you want and real talk I can see why," Saint jabbed. "That's some real good pussy." He continued trying to get a rise out of Dayvid.

"Get to the point?" Dayvid finally chimed in.

"Haha," Saint laughed knowing he touched a nerve. "I gotcha money and I gotcha bitch. Now the money is mine, I figure that makes us even for the shit you and your sisters got out the storage spot a year or so ago, you feel me. But what I wanna know is how much you love ya bitch?" Saint questioned, then paused waiting for an answer.

"What you waiting for me to beg you to let her go?" Dayvid said calmly. "If you was gonna let her go you would've done it already. So what you want Slim? You got Nova and you got my bread but you called me, so what's up?"

"I just wanna know if you love her enough to die for her? Cause that's what has to happen to make all this right. Somebody gotta die, your choice. You want your bitch to live, you gotta come trade your life for hers. No way around it. I'll be at the auto shop on North Avenue, you got an hour." Saint informed him then hung up.

Saint pulled up to the shop in East Baltimore and drove around the back. He owned the place and used it to fix the vehicles he used for his cash rental business. It was a perfect place to hold Nova since they were closed on Sunday's. He came to a stop in front of one of the garage doors and honked his horn. The door slowly began to lift up and he pulled his BMW in as Jaz let the door down behind him. Pharaoh's truck was parked just across from his and Nova's sat next to it. Saint stepped out, slamming the door behind him and bopped across the shop in his signature strut. Pharaoh and his men stood over a battered Droop, who was balled up on the floor, his clothes covered in a mixture of blood, oil and grease. One man was kicking and stomping him while Pharaoh stood laughing with a crowbar in his hand. Both men turned their attention to Saint as he approached.

"Look at chu," Saint said squatting down next to Droop. "On your belly like the snake you are."

"I don't know what the fuck you talking bout, my nigga," Droop said with blood dripping from his mouth. "You got it all fucked up! Whatever it is you thinking, you wrong my nigga."

Chuckling a bit as he rose to his feet, Saint let him in on the reason he was there. "Oh, I'm wrong huh? So, you didn't put King Dayvid on to me and my whereabouts to save your own ass?" Saint quizzed.

"Nah, my nigga it wasn't me, maybe it was one of these niggas," he said trying to shift the blame. "You know these B-more niggas all stick together," he claimed, only to be hit with the crowbar by Pharaoh.

"Nah, it was you Droop," Saint said with a menacing smile picking up a large chain from off the floor. "You wanna know how I know? Taj told me…yeah, your baby moms, who by the way gives the best head I've ever had," Saint mocked grabbing his dick sharing a laugh with the rest of the men in the room. The look on Droop's face spoke a million words. "Yeah nigga," Saint taunted.

"Fuck you," Droop shouted.

"Nah, Fuck you," Saint replied followed by multiple blows with the chain in his hand. Blood splattered everywhere as Saint delivered the beating leaving him covered in Droop's blood. "Yo string this nigga up," he said to Jaz and the one of Pharaoh's henchmen.

The two men lifted Droop off the floor and hooked him to an engine lift, elevating him off the ground slightly, suspending him in air.

"Where's the bitch?" Saint asked Pharaoh referring to Nova.

"She's in the office," he replied.

"Go get her, I want her to see this," Saint said as he removed his shirt and picked up the propane blow torch on top of a tool chest.

Pharaoh wheeled Nova out the shop's office. She was duct taped to the office chair and her mouth had a strip over it as well. The panic in her eyes seeing Saint standing in the middle of the shop, covered in blood holding a blow torch, spoke volumes. The sinister look on his face sent a chill up her spine and she was overtaken with fear.

"What's up Nova, I want you to have a front row seat. So you can see what will happen to you if Dayvid don't show up," Saint declared.

He turned his attention back to Droop, ripping the front of his shirt open, exposing his bare chest. The sound of the blow torch cutting on was like music to Saint's ear. But the sight of the blue flame made Droop start screaming before it ever touched his flesh.

The blood curdling cry Droop let out as Saint scorched his skin with the flame made Nova look away unable to take the gruesome sight of the charred and blistering flesh. Saint stopped briefly, looking down at the floor at the puddle of urine beneath where Droop hung, he burst into laughter. "This nigga done pissed and shit on himself, son."

The rest of the men joined in the laughter.

Saint returned the flame to his skin, this time on his face. "Arrgh! Oh God," Droop called out, the pain too much to withstand.

"Don't be yelling to God now nigga," Saint ridiculed.

The side of Droop's face began to bubble and the seared smell of burnt flesh and feces filled the air of the auto shop making Nova sick to her stomach. Droop stopped screaming after a while and Pharaoh finally spoke up.

"Yo G, I think that nigga dead."

* * *

U.S. Marshals Torrence and Palmeri managed to stay close but out of sight as they tailed Saint through the streets of Baltimore. Following him for almost 2 hours as he made drop-offs wasn't exactly what Palmeri had in mind. He felt like they had been chasing their tail. Turning on North Avenue they observed him pulling into the parking lot of a closed auto shop and parked across the street with a perfect line of sight to the front of the building.

"We need to see what's going on inside that building," Torrence said in frustration. Chasing the fugitive family across the country had taken a serious toll on her physically and mentally. Something that hadn't gone unnoticed by her partner.

"Have you been sleeping any, Roni?" Palmeri asked ignoring her statement. "You look like shit," he scoffed.

"Fuck you. It's none of your business," she snapped back.

"My ass is on the line out here every time we step out this car. I need to know you are clicking on all cylinders and have my back. Whether you care to or not, I want to make it back home at night," Palmeri explained.

"I'm just fine. Now we need to see what's going on inside that building."

"He's a drug dealer Roni, what do you think is going on inside there," Palmeri sarcastically stated. "I'm not here to make any drug bust. I'm here because you said this will lead us to the Porters somehow. So unless Fallon or Autumn are inside, I could give two shits what's happening in there," Palmeri said as he leaned his seat back and closed his eyes. "Wake me up when you see some movement."

Torrence let out a long sigh. "You're a fucking asshole."

"Thank you."

True be told, a stakeout wasn't what she had hoped for either. Torrence's gut was telling her she was on the right path and in her 16 years in law enforcement that feeling had never deceived her.

Renee was the key to locating the Porters, Torrence knew it and Saint was the key to getting vital information on Renee. *Maybe this is where he keeps all the drugs,* she thought to herself. *If we can bust in and catch him we'll have leverage and can make him tell us what he knows.* Now she just had to convince her partner it was worth the risk.

The pedestrian traffic on the block was unusually busy for a Sunday, Torrence noticed as she assessed the landscape, trying to weigh her options. Too many innocent lives had been affected in the government's pursuit of the Porters. But Torrence was drowning in despair and bordering insanity. Her lack of sleep made her irrational and willing to go to any limits to not feel defeated by the lawless siblings.

* * *

Dayvid careened up the block with a wobble in his gait, his face and clothes covered in filth. The raggedy beard, ripped sweat suit, fingerless gloves, oversized beanie and worn out sneakers he wore, blended in perfectly with the many crack and heroin addicts scouring up and down the block for their next fix. Dayvid sold it well, scratching fiercely pretending to suffer from earlier stages of withdrawal. He had spent many nights as a child studying the movements of junkies on his block from his bedroom window and had all the mannerisms down. Convincingly, Dayvid was able to stagger past the two U.S. Marshals staked out in an unmarked car in front of the auto shop, unnoticed. Assuming them to be nothing more than local detectives trying to build a case on Saint and his crew or at the most feds trying to do the same. Dayvid had no idea he was standing only a few feet from the woman who was the Porters arch enemy and had chased his sisters all over the country trying to bring them to justice.

Dayvid crossed the street and around the back of the shop. Banging on the door he waited for a few seconds. He could hear the chains start to move as the door slowly began to lift up. Three guns pointed directly at him when he was in complete view, the exact greeting he thought he would receive. Dayvid raised his arms to his side and allowed for one of the men to search him.

"He clean!" the young man yelled over his shoulder.

"Bring that nigga over here!" Saint shouted his adrenaline pumping and his chest heaving up and down. Saint grabbed Nova's chair and slid her to him, spinning her around.

Nova's head was still spinning from being hit in the head with Pharaoh's gun. She had dried up blood on the back of her head, down her neck and the lights from the auto shop weren't helping much. Nova slowly tried to relax her eyes from squinting and focused on the men walking towards her. Nova's heart skipped a beat when her eyes landed on the man being led towards her at gun point. Through the overgrown, ungroomed beard and tattered clothes, underneath all the dirt she could still see Dayvid as clear as day. It was his eyes; in those eyes she saw the man she loved with every fiber in her body and hated with everything in her at the same time. *How could this be? He's really alive,* she said to herself. The struggle of emotions inside of her were overwhelming. Looking at him walking towards her felt like a weird, sick dream, one that she had experienced on many of nights after hearing of his death.

Dayvid stared in her eyes trying to gage her reaction, but through the terrified look on her face it was hard to read how she felt about seeing him again. Instead he decided to offer her some reassurance that everything would be okay.

"Everything is gonna be aight," he said as he was brought to a stop a few feet from her.

Nova just looked away, breaking eye contact with him.

"She don't look happy to see you, my nigga," Saint taunted. "Let me help you out," he continued before grabbing Nova's face and forcing her to look back at Dayvid. "Dayvid is here because I offered him the chance to trade his life for yours. I'm not sure how much that really means since he's supposed to be dead already. But either way that's some romantic shit," he laughed then snatched the tape from over Nova's mouth.

"No, Dayvid don't do this!" Nova shouted as tears formed in the wells of her eyes. She couldn't lose him twice. She knew she wasn't strong enough to go through it all over again. She would rather die with him. "You can't trust him, Dayvid!"

"You can trust this, one of y'all are not walking out of here," Saint declared.

"I see you grew some nuts since the last time I saw you slim," Dayvid said glaring at Saint with a deathly cold look in his eyes. "You got a lot more mouth, than I remember."

Saint pulled the gun from the small of his back and pointed it at Dayvid. "Yeah, this what the fuck I got to say nigga." The game had come full circle for the two men, now it was Saint in a position of power. He wanted to see the fear King Dayvid had instilled in so many exuding from him. But Dayvid showed no such fear, he had come to trade his life for the woman he loved. He had once told Nova, he would give his life twice for her and Dayvid was prepared to do just that. He was steadfast in his loyalty to her and now he was willing to make the ultimate sacrifice.

"You waving that gun around supposed to scare me?" Dayvid asked calmly. "Just let her go and let's get to it.

"Get on your knees muthafucka," Saint said moving closer to Dayvid and pressing the gun up against his forehead. "Get on your knees and beg for your life," Saint shouted with a crazed look in his eye.

"I don't bend knees for nobody but God, Slim. If you're gonna kill me, you're gonna kill me on my feet."

"Get this nigga on his knees," Saint ordered spit flying from his mouth.

Pharaoh hit Dayvid in the middle of his back with the butt of his gun, followed by another blow that finally dropped him. Seeing Dayvid on his knees, Saint struck him across the face with his gun sending blood spewing from his mouth. Nova screamed as Saint struck him again.

Dayvid wiped the blood from his mouth and smirked. "So this is what the city has come to huh, Pharaoh? Ya'll let an out of town nigga come out here and dictate to you. Y'all that weak? I remember when we used to send niggas like this back up north in a body bag. Now you doing his dirty work, sucking his dick for a living," Dayvid laughed. "I'd rather be dead."

The force of the blow from Pharaoh's foot sent him to the ground flat on his stomach, knocking the wind out of him. "Fuck you nigga, you talking that B-More shit. You took from your own. You and your sisters robbed every nigga in the city," Pharaoh barked.

"I can't blame you Slim, a nigga like you ain't never seen no real money. What's ya split, 50-50?" Dayvid asked. "Nah, dumb nigga like you ain't getting 50 percent of shit. You look like a 10 percent nigga. 10 percent of 1.5 is good, for a nigga like you."

"1.5?" Pharaoh asked turning to Saint perplexed. "What this nigga talking bout?"

Caught off guard, Saint was at a loss for words. "This nigga just talking son, he saying anything to save his ass."

"He telling the truth!" Nova screamed. "The money is in my trunk."

"Fuck this," Saint yelled. "Kill this bitch too," he ordered one of Pharaoh's henchmen.

"Hold up," Pharaoh shouted. "Nah, don't move. Let the lady talk," he said to his henchmen.

Saint pointed his gun at the henchmen "You heard what I said, kill this bitch."

"Nah nigga, you heard what I said?" Pharaoh cocked his gun and aimed it at Saint. "You the snake, you holding out on me."

Saint turned pointing his gun back at him. "Hold up nigga, I was gonna break bread with you," Saint lied. "You my nigga, you know I got you."

"I just watched you torture and kill ya so called nigga. So you can miss me wit' that."

BANG!

The distinct sound of a gun going off caught U.S. Marshal Torrence's attention immediately. "Angelo!" she yelled frantically waking her partner from his nap. "Shots fired!" she screamed jumping from the car, pulling her weapon from her holster and zig zagging through oncoming traffic as cars honked at her.

"Roni!" Palmeri called out trying to stop her to no avail. "Fuck!" he said to himself opening the door and taking off after her.

The shot reverberated throughout the auto shop as everyone ducked for cover. The side of Saint's head exploded like a smashed watermelon and brain matter splattered everywhere as he collapsed to the ground. Blood leaked from his head forming a red stream spilling from his body. Jaz, Pharaoh's henchmen, stood over Saint holding his gun.

"I hate New York niggas," he voiced as he picked up the keys to Nova's car from next to Saint's lifeless body.

"That's what I'm talking bout lil nigga," Pharaoh bragged, singing his youngin's praises. "Now let's kill these muthafuckas, get that money and get the fuck outta here."

"No doubt," Jaz said. "But we ain't leaving here together," he informed the rotund hustler aiming his weapon at him. "Even in school, I never was good with division," he said squeezing the trigger, hitting Pharaoh once in the chest and once in the shoulder.

"U.S. Marshals, nobody move!" Veronica Torrence screamed.

Jaz turned and fired at her. The other henchmen fired several shots at her as well. Torrence took cover from the haul of bullets. Dayvid raced towards Nova, who was still duct taped to the chair in the middle of the shop with bullets whizzing all around her.

"Dayvid!" she cried out.

"I got you," he assured Nova pulling her out of harm's way, while picking up Saint's gun off the floor.

"Dayvid," Torrence thought to herself hearing the woman's screams. *No way.* She tried her best to get a look at the homeless man but his back was to her.

Palmeri burst through the door returning fire at Jaz and the other gunman. "Roni, you ok?"

"Yes," she shouted as she popped up and joined in the gun battle.

Palmeri struck Jaz's partner with two bullets dropping him. Jaz took off running, Palmeri gave chase while continuing to fire at the young gunner.

Dayvid quickly released Nova from her restraints and she leaped from the chair, wrapping her arms around his neck, almost squeezing the life out of him ignoring the crud he was covered in. "Not now, we gotta get outta here."

"What about the money?" she questioned.

"Fuck it, I'll just have to figure something out," Dayvid said grabbing her hand and running towards the emergency exit.

Nova ran as fast as she could trying to keep up with him. Finally, they reached the door and Dayvid pushed it open setting off the alarm. Nova raced through the door while he held it open.

"Dayvid Porter!" Torrence shouted. "Don't move you're under arrest."

Hearing his name called made Dayvid's heart skip a beat, realizing that his cover had been blown. Turning he saw the familiar face of the Marshal that brought him the news about Rain while he was in North Branch. *This bitch,* he thought. Without hesitation, Dayvid lifted his gun and began walking towards her and firing. Torrance had no choice but to dive for cover. Dayvid then hauled ass out the exit. A few second later Palmeri came rushing around the corner out of breath with his gun drawn but he was too late.

"My guy got away," he said trying to suck in some air. "Who was the bum with the girl?" he asked, helping Torrence up off the ground.

"That," she paused getting to her feet and dusting herself off. "That was Dayvid Porter," she announced. "He's alive."

Palmeri stood there bewildered, her revelation had confounded his thoughts and rendered his tongue useless.

12

"Hatred stirs up dissension; But love covers all transgressions." - *Proverbs 10:12*

Dayvid and Nova maneuvered their way through the block as quickly as possible towards the Ford Explorer Dayvid parked a block away from the scene. Earlier that day he paid a visit to Miss Jackie and sat with her for a couple of hours explaining all that had taken place. He asked her about him and Rain's biological father. Dayvid wanted to know what made Miss Jackie so sure that after explaining to David Banks that the Porter twins were his kids, he would help.

Miss Jackie's reply was, "One thing I know for sure was that, that man loved your mother just as much or even more than she loved him. It had to be something out of his control or without his knowledge that would keep them apart."

Miss Jackie and Dayvid conversed some more while Dayvid explained the proposition given to him by Saint. She asked if there was anything she could do to help but Dayvid would have none of it. He wasn't sure if his plan would work but if it did, he would need a reliable vehicle to get him and Nova out of town. Miss Jackie, without hesitation, offered her 2005 Ford Explorer. She rarely drove it, preferring to walk, but she kept it running good and it would definitely get them where they needed to go.

Nova was out of breath and feeling dizzy from the blood loss she had from her head wound, Dayvid opened the passenger side of the car and sat her inside. Dayvid got in the driver's side and immediately sped off. He knew it wouldn't be long before the U.S Marshals would be on his ass, or the backup they most certainly called would catch wind of the speeding vehicle. When Dayvid got at least six blocks away he slowed down to normal speed trying to remain undetected. Nova sat in the passenger seat quietly, nothing was heard but the sniffling from her nose. The tears flowed from her eyes and the silent whimpers left her mouth. She could not believe the turn of events in her life for the past six months. She had lost love, regained it and lost it again. Now she was sitting next to a ghost. Dayvid looked over at Nova and reached his hand over to wipe the tears off her cheek. Nova moved away from his touch, unsure of how she felt about him at that moment. She was on the verge of losing her life and Dayvid had come to the rescue like he always did. But she was still upset, if he hadn't faked his death and left her for self, she would have never met and fell for a nigga like Saint. Dayvid knew with him in the picture there would have never been any room for another man in her heart.

"I know you got a lot of questions. I promise you as soon as we get to where we need to be, I'll answer everything."

Nova stared at Dayvid, who was now focused on the road. She studied his appearance and how different he looked. Nova knew what he wore was a disguise but she could see deeper than the ripped and ragged clothes or even the dirt spots he wore on his face. Nova saw a man who had been through some things that the mind could not fathom. But so had she.

"For six months I thought you were gone," she spoke solemnly. "Six whole months a part of me was empty, missing, I felt ripped apart. I had to rebuild myself, figure out who and where I wanted to be. And all I was left with was a one page letter and a key," she said as her voice began to rise and crack. "What were you going through that I couldn't be a part of Dayvid? I would've gone to the end of God's earth with you, and straight to hell after. But you closed me out, lied to me, and you left me alone. Now all you can say after all this time is you know I have questions."

Nova sat upright in her seat and positioned herself to face Dayvid. In order for her to feel any kind of happiness at that very moment, she had to let out all of her resentment. Dayvid stared straight ahead at the road. He did not say a word, instead just listened. Nova was hurting and he was the blame.

"I've cried myself to sleep, swept the hair off the bathroom floor that I've loss due to stress. Not having you in my life was the hardest thing I have ever had to deal with. I mean what the fuck Dayvid! You couldn't find me, warn me or tell me something? Huh? Look at me, did you even bother to look? Answer me!" Nova shouted in anger, spit flew out of her mouth while she spoke. At that point she needed answers and she wasn't about to oblige him by waiting until they got to wherever they were going to get them.

"I did look for you Nova. I turned down the chance for a clean slate and fresh start, to look for you. Because I promised you one. Fuck you think I've been beasting in these streets tryna eat, trying to figure out where you were so we could get the fuck out of here. It was hard to find you tho, cause you was with your man." Dayvid spewed back with jealousy and anger. Nova had a right to feel the way she did and demand answers to her questions, but it hurt Dayvid to the core to know she would feel he would willingly abandon her. He only wanted Nova to move on if something was to have happened to him. But to be alive and well and know that she was in bed with his adversary gave him a sick feeling in his stomach. Saint was a weak nigga, not even close to the caliber of a man he was so it bothered him that she had been with him. But deep down inside he knew it was his fault. He had pushed Nova into the arms of another man and truly couldn't be mad at her.

"I would've never...if I would've known...I," emotions and tears had her tongue tied. Although Dayvid was supposed to be dead in her eyes and she did not know the history between him and Saint, she still felt as if she had betrayed him, breaking their bond. Her heart sunk into her stomach. "What was I supposed to do? I'm sorry," was all Nova could say.

Dayvid grabbed the back of her head, pulling her towards him. "No, I'm sorry, you don't have anything to apologize to me for."

Nova unclamped her seatbelt and snuggled up as close to her man as possible while he drove.

"Don't worry about nothing, it's all over. I'm here, you're safe, and we back," Dayvid reassured, letting her know everything was going to be fine. All he wanted was to get out the game, make Nova his wife and have some kids. He never imagined any of it happening the way it had. But now that he had a second chance, he would not allow anything or anyone to ruin it.

Nova ran her hand over his chest and down his leg taking in his presence. "You're really here, I thought I lost you," Nova said in a soft tone.

"Yeah, I'm here and I ain't going nowhere else without you. I promise."

Nova closed her eyes attempting to rest. Before she drifted off to sleep Nova whispered his name.

"Dayvid."

"Wassup," he replied.

"Where are we going?" she asked.

"Miami. We going to Miami. I know somebody out there that can help get us to Mexico."

* * *

"I know what I saw Angelo," Torrence said as they stepped on to the elevator. "This has nothing to do with my lack of sleep," she insisted as the two of them rode the hospital elevator up to the 8th floor.

The two Marshals moved quickly down the hallway until they reached room 8031. They entered without knocking and were greeted by a nurse in the room.

"Hey, you can't be in here," she said. "Who are you?"

Torrence and Palmeri both flashed their badges and explained who they were and why they were there. The nurse was reluctant but eventually agreed to let them speak to her patient.

"I have some more rounds to make and when I come back, I want you two gone. I don't care what those badges say," she said every word dripping with sass as she switched out of the room.

"How are you feeling Pharaoh?" Palmeri asked pushing the button on the bed sitting him up.

"How it look like I feel?" he snapped back. "What the fuck y'all want wit me?"

"We won't take up much of your time, just got one quick question," Torrence said. "The man dressed like a bum in the auto

shop, who was that?"

Pharaoh grunted from the pain as he adjusted his position on the bed, "If I told you, you'd think I was crazy."

"Try me," she said.

"That was Dayvid Porter," Pharaoh confessed.

"The Dayvid Porter," Palmeri asked. "Are you sure?"

"Yes, King Dayvid. I'm 100 percent sure."

The two Marshals exited the room heading for the elevator. They had received the confirmation they needed, at least Palmeri, Torrence was already sure of what she had seen. She had looked down the barrel of Dayvid's gun. She didn't need much more confirmation than that.

"Somebody has got some explaining to do," she said as they exited the hospital walking to their car. "How did Dayvid Porter get out of a super max prison? More importantly who helped him?"

"Yeah, something stinks like shit," Palmeri said opening the driver side door. "Let's get back to the office and see what we can dig up."

* * *

"This just in the newsroom here at CNN, we have breaking news. The Federal Bureau of Investigations and the U.S. Marshal's Fugitive Task are all on high alert tonight after it is being reported that Dayvid Porter, the only male member of the infamous Porter clan is said to be alive and at large. You may remember the reports months ago that Porter had committed suicide while locked in North Branch Correctional Institute, a federal facility outside of Baltimore. It is now being reported that he faked his death in order to escape the super max prison. No other information is available at this time as to his whereabouts but law enforcement officials warn that he is to be considered armed and extremely dangerous. If you see him, you are advised to contact your local law enforcement and do not approach him. We reached out to officials at the prison where he was being held and we were told that they have launched a full investigation into the incident and circumstances leading to this breach of security. We will be updating you as more information becomes available."

* * *

Entering Miami-Dade County

Dayvid pulled the Explorer into the parking lot of the Knights Inn on Biscayne Boulevard in North Miami. He had been to Miami enough times to know exactly where he and Nova could lay low until he was able to get in contact with the person that could help get them to Mexico. It had been a year or so since they had spoken but Dayvid knew just how to get in contact with him. First, he needed to get Nova settled so he could hit the streets.

"Nov," he called her name. "Nov, wake up we're here baby," he said tapping her.

Nova opened her eyes and began to stretch. She had a crick in her neck from leaning against the door while sleep throughout the long ride. They had stopped in Savannah at a waffle house but outside of quick stops for gas they had drove straight through the night. Nova was hungry and she couldn't wait to get out the car to stretch her legs. Looking at the hotel they were parked in front of she thought to herself how the rundown spot was what she exactly had in mind when she heard Miami. "It's not the Fontainebleau, but it will do," she joked.

Dayvid just smiled. "I need you to go in and get the room. They not gonna ask you for id, they'll take cash," he told her as he peeled a few dollars of his thin knot.

"That's all the money we've got?" she asked noticing his limited funds.

"Yeah, for now but I don't plan on us being here long. I gotta go holla at somebody," Dayvid informed her.

Nova took the money and headed inside to the office of the hotel. After a few minutes she emerged holding a room key in her hand.

Walking into the room, Nova headed straight for the bed and jumped on it, letting out a sigh of relief. She was exhausted and wasn't concern about the look of the room in the 2-star hotel. Dayvid closed the door behind him and sat on the bed next to her. He was wired and didn't feel the need to sleep. He was going to rest easy anyway not until he at least secured them a way to Mexico. He had heard the reports on the radio while he was driving and knew every police officer in the country was looking for him.

"I'm about to make a run," he said while rubbing her leg.

"You don't want to take a shower and change first?" she asked turning up her nose up teasing him. "You stink," she laughed.

"So does your breath," Dayvid teased her back putting his hand over his nose. "I'll be back in no time."

Nova sat up on the bed, her nerves were still jumpy. She didn't want to let him out of her sight, after losing him once she was scared of losing him again.

Dayvid saw the look on her face and rubbed his hand against the side of her face, then played with her hair. "I like your new look," he said then smiled showing his beautiful set of teeth and dimples. "I'll be right back, I promise," he assured her looking directly into her eyes.

Dayvid drove through the industrial park in Hialeah Gardens searching for Lupita's, the Mexican restaurant owned by the leader of one of the biggest drug cartels in the country. Dayvid parked in front, headed inside and took a seat at a table near the back. After a few minutes, a young Mexican girl came to his table to take his order.

"Hello senor, may I take your order?" she asked with a smile on her face.

Dayvid looked up at the young girl and said, "lo que quiero no está en el menu," pushing the menu to the side.

The young girl had a look of confusion on her face. "No

entiendo lo que quieres decir," she said not understanding his request.

"Gallardo," Dayvid said.

The young girl disappeared into the back of the restaurant, after a few seconds a bald head Mexican man, dressed in a polo shirt and slacks approached Dayvid's table.

"How may I help you, senor?" he asked.

"Gallardo," Dayvid repeated.

"And who might you be?" he asked.

"El Rey."

The man's eyes opened wide as a four-lane highway, he definitely knew the name, King, but had never laid his eyes on the man whose name instilled fear and the hearts of many. "Un minuto," the man said disappearing into the back of the restaurant. After about 15 minutes, the kitchen doors opened, and a man signaled for Dayvid to follow him.

Dayvid walked through the kitchen and was led down a flight of stairs into the cellar of the restaurant. Standing in the middle of the room, surrounded by a group of Mexican henchmen, was Avila Gallardo— the exotically beautiful and glamourous leader of the Mala Lobos Cartel. The 42-year-old woman looked better than women half her age and was as deadly as men twice her size. She had used Dayvid's services plenty of times to get rid of potential problems. He never missed a target, something she loved about him. Plus, he was easy on the eyes; at least he usually was. He could tell by the look on her face that his appearance was throwing her for a loop.

"King Dayvid, my handsome friend," she said in her thick, sexy Spanish accent. "What happened to you?" she asked.

"Long story," he said with a charming smile.

"I been watching you on the television. First, you're dead," she paused. "Then you're not dead, it's very entertaining," said the sultry queen pin. "But what I want to know is what you are doing here?"

"I need your help," Dayvid confessed. "I know you know my situation and I need to get to Mexico as soon as possible, me and my girlfriend. I know you can make that happen…"

"No, no, no, no, no," she shook her head and frowned her lips. "You are way too hot to touch. My organization doesn't need that type of heat. You have every law enforcement agency in the country after you and you come here, to me!" she shouted in anger. "I should shoot you right now, just for coming here."

"You know I wouldn't have come here, if I had any other choice. I just figured we've done a lot of business together and we have history. I thought…"

"And you thought that meant something," she finished his sentence before a long pause. "Well King Dayvid," she said letting his name roll off her tongue. "You're in luck, I'm willing to help you."

"Thank you, Avila. I appreciate it."

"Don't thank me so soon," she informed him. "Might I remind

you, nothing in this world is free," she said walking towards him. "I had a couple of my guys go missing with something that belongs to me. 20 keys," she proclaimed. "You find my keys, you bring em back and I'll put you and your girlfriend on a cargo ship tomorrow evening. You'll be in Mexico, just like that," she snapped her fingers for emphasis.

Dayvid, with no other choice, agreed to her terms. Avila handed him a phone and told him she would contact him later. Then had her men escorted him out.

* * *

Dayvid used the room key to open the door, upon entering the room he saw Nova laying on the bed in a tight wife beater and some panties. Her hair was wet and curly from being washed and left to air dry and she looked beautiful in her natural state. Dayvid stood with his back against the door admiring the love of his life. For a while he thought he had lost Nova and to see her laying there peacefully with her eyes closed brought a calm over him. It made everything he had been through over the past few months, worth it. Dayvid placed the car keys on the nightstand and headed over to the bed.

Nova opened her eyes and smiled when she felt Dayvid's presence in the room. "Hey baby," her voice cracked from the sleep she was just in.

"Wassup, you good?" Dayvid rubbed her thigh, leaned over and kissed her butt cheek.

Nova smiled and rubbed the top of his head. "Never been better."

"I got some shit I got to handle for my peoples," he informed her. "Once I'm done, we outta here."

"What do you mean handle?" she questioned. "Is it safe? Are you gonna be okay?" her voice full of concern.

"It'll be cool," he said calmly not wanting to worry her. "We gonna be good. We been through too much already. I ain't gonna let nothing happen.

Nova sat up on the bed and mounted Dayvid on his lap, wrapping her legs around his waist. She put her hands on the top of his head and kissed his lips softly. "I just want us to be happy Dayvid. Happy and safe," she stated resting her head against his.

"And we will, I promise. I do this shit and it gets us on a cargo ship to Mexico," he told her. "You know there's nothing I wouldn't do to make sure we straight, I love you Nov," Dayvid reassured.

"I know you do, and for you I will do whatever it takes."

"So will I."

"Okay, so can you do one small thing for me now tho?" she asked sheepishly.

"What's that?" Dayvid replied playfully tickling her.

"Can you go in there and wash your ass because you stink man!"

They both bust out laughing, Dayvid smacked Nova on the ass

and pushed her back on the bed.

"Ha, I'm on it," Dayvid leaped up heading towards the bathroom to shower.

Before he could turn on the water Nova yelled out, "Hey I got you some razors and deodorant. Maybe you can shave that scruffy shit off your face. You're looking like wolverine!" Nova got up from the bed and reached in the bag with the stuff she bought earlier at the gas station. They didn't have a big variety to pick from, but she was able to get some much needed toiletries and some candles. She had hopes on creating a half-way romantic mood in the two-star motel they were in. It had been a long time since she been with her man and although they both had been through some fucked up shit, she needed to feel him. Tonight, she planned on reconnecting with the love of her life mentally, emotionally and physically.

"I been in grind mode, stack and starve. I ain't have time for nothing else. But just because you asked, I got you. How you get all this shit anyway?" Dayvid yelled from in the shower.

"Whatever, just go in there and bring my man back out, please," she teased. "I went to the gas station across the street earlier, I needed to get out this room" Nova replied while she lit the candles.

"You gotta be cool, we are on the run," he said slightly unhappy with her decision.

"I was," she snapped back.

Dayvid stood in the shower, letting the water run over his head. He thought about how after so much had went wrong, he felt blessed to have Nova back by his side and the opportunity to make everything right again. Stepping out the shower, he walked over to the mirror and used one of the towels to wipe the fog off the mirror so he could see his reflection. "Damn you do look crazy slim," he said to himself. He grabbed the razor and went to work.

After about twenty minutes of him being in the bathroom with the water off Nova became impatient. She knocked then opened the bathroom to see what was taking him so long. She smiled seeing the sexy man she fell in love with staring into the mirror.

"You always did clean up nice," Nova complemented. Dayvid was back to his old self, lined up and smelling good. The sight of him made Nova's nipples harden. She walked up behind him, wrapped her arms around his waist and laid her head on his broad shoulders.

"I missed you," she confessed.

Dayvid turned around and picked her up, placing her on the sink. "Show me."

They both locked lips passionately, welcoming each other's tongues in their mouths. It was instant electricity between the two of them. Anxious to feel him inside of her, Nova reached for her panties, trying to pull them down. Dayvid moved her hand and ripped them off with one tug.

"I'll buy you new ones," he said between licks and kisses, while lifting her up and carrying her to the bed. He was anxious to feel her. He missed her touch, her scent, her feel.   Putting Nova on her back, Dayvid placed her legs on his shoulders and kissed her lotus flower softly. He sucked and licked as if he was speaking to it, letting it know how much he missed it. Nova moaned from the extreme pleasure. Wanting to show her gratitude, she sat up on the bed quickly breaking Dayvid out of his rhythm and reached for his rock hard shaft, placing it in her mouth fast and aggressively.

"I missed you Dayvid, I missed him," she said kissing the head.

Dayvid threw his head back enjoying her oral skills. Feeling like he would bust at any moment, he pushed her head away from his dick. He stood there for a few seconds with his thick wood in his hand admiring her. They were both in the heat of the moment and wanted nothing more than to devour one another, but Dayvid knew he needed to take his time reuniting with his queen. Nova understood his feelings without him having to say a word and laid down on her back. He trailed kisses from the heel of her foot to the nape of her neck before entering her wetness. The thickness of his love stick made Nova hold her breath as he entered her. A single tear dropped from the corner of her eye as she felt instantly reconnected to him. Dayvid held onto her shoulders while she wrapped her legs tightly around him. He gave her long, strong strokes until she creamed all on him. They made love for the better part of the night until they both collapsed into a deep sleep.

* * *

The loud thud of the stack of papers being slammed on his desk startled Angelo Palmeri. He was already neck high in unfinished paperwork from the incident at the auto shop and more was the last thing he wanted to see.

"You're going to flip out when you see this," Torrence said with excitement in her voice. "We got forensics from the crime scene. Have you even seen blood with no owner?" she asked flipping open the top folder. "The blood work we did on the blood we know belongs to Dayvid, came back as non-existent. No match in the system, it's like he doesn't exist."

"Really," he said, she now had his full attention. "Somebody went out of their way to make sure Dayvid Porter disappeared off the grid. Who has that type of power?"

"That's the million dollar question but I got something else," she said as her eyes lit up. Torrence flipped open another folder. "We've got a hit on some more blood at the scene. The woman we have been watching and referring to as Renee Preston, is actually Nova James. She's the longtime girlfriend of Dayvid Porter."

"Roni!"

Torrence turned hearing her name being called from across the room. Racing towards her with a piece of paper in his hand was one of the computer techs.

"Roni!" he screamed again as he raced frantically towards her. "We've got a hit on a credit card at a convenience store in Miami."

The two agents grabbed their jackets and raced out the office.

13

"And now these three remain: faith, hope and love. But the greatest of these is love." *-1 Corinthians 13:13*

Dayvid sprinted up the block with his gun in his hand and the heavy duffle bag draped over his shoulder, bouncing off his hip with every step. He could hear the sirens getting closer and knew he needed to get to his truck as quickly as possible. As he turned the corner a police car zoomed by him then slammed on it brakes. The loud screeching sound echoed through the block. Dayvid turned on a dime and let off a few shots in the patrol cars direction before dashing up the block to the Explorer. Dayvid opened the driver side door, tossed the bag onto the passenger seat and jumped in the truck all in one motion. He started the car and slammed down on the gas and sped up the block. As he neared the light on the corner, he saw two police cars parked at the intersection trying to block his path. Dayvid tapped on the break as he turned the wheel, fishtailing in the turn. The back of his truck slammed into the side of one of the police cars, Dayvid hit the gas and sped off with one cop car in pursuit. The police officer proved to be no match for the driving skills of King Dayvid as he maneuvered through the street avoiding them like a game of Pac-Man.

Dayvid put some distance between him and the cops, then turned down a block in a neighborhood and slammed on the brakes. He grabbed the duffle bag, threw it over his shoulder once again and jumped out the truck. Now on foot, he cut through a few backyards as he navigated his way through the neighborhood blocks trying to get as far away from the Explorer as he could. He could hear the sirens in the distance, the more he ran the further away they sounded.

Completely out of wind and sweating profusely from the hot Miami sun, Dayvid stopped momentarily to catch his breath. He looked down at his watch checking the time, after a few minutes he came from around the side of a house and calmly walked up the block.

Dayvid approached the backdoor of Lupita's and knocked. As the door swung open a gun was the first thing Dayvid was greeted with. But the man quickly lowered his weapon seeing Dayvid's face. He quickly ushered him in and slammed the door behind him then led him through the kitchen and out into the empty restaurant.

Avila Gallardo sat by the bar flirting with the handsome young bartender, as he prepared her a drink. Seeing Dayvid enter the room, she immediately turned her attention to him.

"Now that's a fine looking man," she complimented with a smile at his cleaned up look. "Much better than last time," she said in her thick accent. "Since you're here, I'll take that to mean you have a lil' something for me," she said seductively like she always did when talking to him. She had a thing for younger men and wanted nothing more than to rumble in the sheets at least once with Dayvid Porter.

Dayvid hesitated not sure if it was cool to talk in front of the bartender but proceeded when Avila gave him a nod. "Yeah I got it right here," he said tossing the bag on top of the bar.

"Everything here?" she asked raising an eyebrow at him before peeking into the bag.

Dayvid just gave her a look as to say, "What do you think?"

"I kid, I kid. Would you like a drink Mr. Porter?" Avila asked. "I can have Javier whip you up anything you'd like."

"Hennessey, no ice," Dayvid said.

Avila ordered the bartender to fix Dayvid's drink, while she unzipped the bag and began removing the keys. Stacking them on the table, she only counted out 16 keys. "Where's the rest it supposed to be 20?" she asked.

"That was all that was there, "Dayvid informed her. "But check again."

Avila gave him a look and then reached in the bag once more. She felt a plastic bag at the bottom of the duffle bag. Removing it, she placed it on the bar and opened it up seeing what looked to be about 100 thousand dollars in cash. Her eyes opened wide in surprise.

"That's the cash they had on them too," said Dayvid.

The smile on her face said it all as she thumbed through the cash. Avila couldn't believe that a man in Dayvid's desperate position could still be so trustworthy. "What a pleasant surprise," Avila boasted.

"Trust is the glue of life. It's an essential part of doing business," Dayvid said as he downed his Hennessy.

"Very true," she replied. Avila grabbed a pen and jotted something down on a napkin before sliding it over to him. "That's all the info you'll need to locate the cargo ship you'll be on."

"Speaking of," Dayvid paused temporarily. "I'm kind of in need of a new ride."

"No problem. Javier give Dayvid your keys," she instructed the young bartender.

Dayvid guided the Nissan Altima through the streets of Miami as fast as he could without drawing unwanted attention from police. He didn't have much time to waste, he needed to pick up Nova and get to the Port of Miami in less than 45 minutes. He knew this was their one and only shot to get out the country. Avila Gallardo had U.S.

Customs, Border Patrol and the Coast Guard all in her pocket breaking them all off a percentage to make sure her cocaine operation ran smooth. Dayvid knew all he had to do was get on the ship to guarantee their safe passage. He had walked through the fires of hell and for the most part came out unscathed. He had Nova back and looked forward to seeing his sisters and starting a new life.

Dayvid pulled out his phone and dialed Nova's number. He needed her to understand the importance of being ready to leave as soon as he arrived. She, like every woman, tended to take forever to get ready. They couldn't afford that today.

Dayvid listened as the phone rang a few times before she picked up.

"Hey babe," she said upon answering the phone. "Where you at?"

"I'm on my way now," he replied. "You ready to leave? I need you all packed up ready to go when I pull up. I just wanna run in, grab a bag and go," he reiterated.

"I'm ready," she said.

"You ready to be Mrs. Porter?" he asked out of nowhere.

"Mrs. Porter?" she asked. He could tell she was smiling. "What are you talking about with your crazy self?"

"I'm talking about you being my wife," he said this time sounding more serious, looking down at the open ring box and diamond ring on his lap. He had bought it months ago anticipating them escaping to Mexico after the big heist. He had asked Miss

Jackie to keep it safe for him and she had given it back to him when he went to visit her. Dayvid visualized a romantic wedding on the beach with Fallon and Autumn as her maid of honors and Rain as his best man.

"You're really serious," Nova said hearing it in his tone. She couldn't help but get emotional. She had loved only him since she was sixteen years old and would always practice writing her name with his last name in hopes that one day it would be a reality. So, to hear him say those word was a dream come true. "Yes, I would love to be your wife Dayvid," she said fighting back tears.

"That's what I needed to hear," he said as a smile stretched wide across his face. "I'll be there in a few minutes," he said.

"Ok, I need to find my Black Album before you get here. I can't leave without it," she said.

"What?" Dayvid asked a bit confused.

"You heard me," she said.

"Ok," he replied. "Nova," he said pausing briefly. "I love you."

Nova smiled as she visualized his handsome face speaking those words. "I love you too, my king. I'll see you soon," she said before hanging up.

"You did the right thing," U.S. Marshal Torrence said to her as she put the phone down.

The two Marshals had Nova in custody inside of her hotel room. The entire hotel was surrounded by F.B.I. Agents and the Fugitive Task Force waiting to capture Dayvid as soon as he showed his face on the property.

"You seem like a descent young lady. You don't need to be mixed up with a ruthless criminal like Dayvid Porter." Palmeri schooled her.

"You don't know anything about me, and you don't know who he really is," Nova said as she sat down on the bed with tears rolling down her cheeks.

"No darling, I think you're the one who doesn't know who he really is," Torrence lectured. "Do you know how many deaths your King and his sisters are responsible for? Consider yourself lucky," she scolded.

Nova just lowered her head and began sobbing.

Dayvid hung up and pulled into the gas station across the street from the Knights Inn. He parked so the he was looking directly at the hotel. As he scanned the parking lot, he was able to easily pick out the unmarked police vehicles, strategically placed around the building with F.B.I and Task Force agents seated in them. Nova had given him the heads by dropping the Black Album clue in their conversation. Still Dayvid sat in his car contemplating what to do. He had gone through hell and back just to be able to bring Nova with him and here he was forced to decide between walking into a trap to save her once again or to leave without her. He knew what Nova would want him to do, her dropping the clue was her answer. She knew they couldn't do anything to her, but they would surely put a needle in his arm if they could. Dayvid stared down at the diamond ring in the box on his lap with tears forming in the wells of his eyes. He felt a lump in his throat as he tried to fight back his tears to no avail. Dayvid looked at the bag of money sitting on his passenger seat, Avila Gallardo gave him the 100 thousand dollars he recovered as a going away present. Reaching in the bag, he grabbed the gun. "I wonder how many agents are in the room with her," he thought with love in his heart and hate in his eyes. He slammed the ring box closed and tossed it in the bag. Putting the gun on his lap he started the Altima and pulled out the gas station. With tears streaming down his face, Dayvid drove away from the hotel instantly feeling guilt and emptiness. He watched the Knights Inn fade farther and farther away in his rearview mirror until it was gone, just like the life he had left behind; along with his queen, Nova.

Torrence and Palmeri paced back and forth in the room waiting for word that Dayvid was on the property and approaching the room. It had been over twenty minutes since Nova had hung up the phone with him and he should have been there by now.

Torrence began to panic. Her whole life was wrapped up in this case. She had missed her daughter's birthday, neglected her sleep and pushed herself to the limit in pursuit of the Porters. She had the perfect trap laid, so she thought, and now something wasn't right.

"What the fuck is taking so long," she snapped looking over at her partner.

"Be cool Roni, he will be here," Palmeri assured her.

A loud bang on the door made the two Marshals pull their guns from the holsters and aim them straight at the door. They slowly moved towards it, ready to apprehend their suspect. Another bang on the door was followed by a voice calling out the Marshal's names.

"That's Rivera," Palmeri said as he unlocked the door and opened it.

Nova breathed a sigh of relief, happy that it wasn't Dayvid at the door. She wasn't sure if he had gotten here clue and even if he did, she know he would still risk trying to save her. Something she was silently praying he didn't do.

"It just came over the scanner that police found a blue Ford Explorer abandoned in Hialeah with Maryland plates." Rivera said stepping into the room.

"Fuck!" Torrence screamed rushing straight towards Nova and grabbing her around the neck. "You sneaky little bitch. You tipped him off. I don't know how you did it, but you did."

"Roni," Palmeri called out. "What the fuck are you doing?" he shouted while Rivera helped pull her off of Nova. "We will find him Roni! Gotdamn it, but you can't do that," he said as he pushed her out the room.

Nova watched as the Marshals exited the room then cracked a smile. "Fuck you bitch."

EPILOUGE

Mexico

Fallon and Autumn stood waving like kids at a parade, full of excitement watching the door of the private jet that had just landed on Romero's personal air strip open and Rain descended the steps. She had added a few pounds to her thin frame, all in the right places. The positive results of no longer ripping and running. Rain bopped towards them followed by a handsome white gentleman, dressed in a suit.

Unable to contain their happiness, Fallon and Autumn took off running towards her; arms stretched wide prepared to smother her with love. The three sisters embraced, not wanting to let each other go. It had been months since Rain had laid eyes on her younger sisters and she was relieved to see that they were doing great and in good spirits. She couldn't help but to notice the beautiful mansion and property they were living on.

"Damn, Dayvid's people is living large out here," she said.

"You mean, my husband is living large out here," Fallon corrected Rain, putting her hand up flashing the big rock on her finger.

"Bitch what! You're married?" Rain asked in shock.

"Yup," Fallon said with a smile. "Baby sis next," she revealed pointing back up to the house at Q standing next to her husband.

"What the fuck is going on here," Rain said laughing.

"Who is that Rain," Autumn questioned pointing at the white gentleman walking up behind her.

"That's me and Dayvid's dad," Rain answered then watched as her sisters' jaws dropped. "Long story."

"Hello ladies, I'm David Banks," he said sticking his hand out to shake theirs. "I've heard so much about you. You girls are even more beautiful in person," he charmed causing both of them to smile.

"I like him already," Fallon blushed. "Let's go inside," she said.

As the group walked towards the house the loud chopping sound of a helicopter caught their attention and they all turned to see it landing in the field just behind them. The blades came to a stop, just as the door opened and an older white man stepped out.

"Who the hell is that?" Rain asked.

"That's my dad, your grandfather, the Honorable Judge Harrison Banks," David Banks said with a sarcastic tone.

"What is he doing here?" she asked knowing the history between the two men.

"It's only one way to find out," he replied.

The group stood waiting as the elderly man made his way over to them.

"What are you doing here dad?" the young Banks inquired.

"I came to see these kids of yours that you've been so willing to throw your entire career away for. So these are the Porters, minus that bastard son of yours," Judge Banks scoffed. "In your blind haste to fulfill your parental responsibilities, you made a lot of mistakes. Now there's an all-out investigation into how Dayvid Porter walked out of a federal prison undetected. Not to mention how he went missing in the database. You've got a couple U.S. Marshals and F.B.I agents digging into how that happened. How long do you think it will take before your name comes up?" he asked rhetorically. "So like usual I'm here to clean up your mess."

By the time everyone heard the shot it was already too late. Rain felt the blood spatter on her face as she watched her father collapse on to his face from a sniper's bullet ripping through the back of his skull.

Fallon and Autumn screamed at the top of their lungs as Rain dropped to her knees lifting her father into her arms. There was no saving him, he was gone. The shot had killed him instantly. Rain was covered in blood as she looked around to see where the shot had come from but was greet by a .40 Cal Beretta being shoved in her face from her grandfather.

"Get up you little dyke bitch," he instructed. "Like I said I'll be damn if I let you black bastards tarnish the Banks name. So I made a deal with some Mexican friends of mine," he said nodding his head back in the direction of the house.

The three sisters turned around to see Romero and Q being held at gun point and the mansion being invaded by men with guns.

"I'm sure you've heard of the Mendoza Cartel," Judge Banks said with a smirk, enjoying the looks on the women's faces.

***

Dayvid's arrival in Mexico was bittersweet. Nova not being by his side returned the empty feeling he had in his heart for all those months. He didn't care what he had to do or how long it would take but he was determined to hold her in his arms once again. His love for her stretched across any border or ocean that was between them. He wouldn't stop until they could be together.

Avila Gallardo kept her word, one of her guys was there to pick him up right off the ship and drive him to Romero's house. After about a forty minute drive, the man dropped Dayvid off at the bottom of a steep hill and pulled off. Dayvid stared up at the long winding hill and saw Romero's crib perched at the top. He couldn't wait to surprise his sisters. It had been too long since he'd seen them and after having to leave Nova in Miami, he needed something to lift his spirits. Seeing the faces of his Porter sibling would do just that, even if only momentarily.

The trek up the steep hill had gotten the best of Dayvid as he was completely exhausted when he reached the top. *Damn, I can't wait to relax for a while,* he thought to himself as he closed his eyes and was almost able feel the cool breeze coming off the water as he chilled on the beaches of Mexico.

The sound of a single gunshot snapped Dayvid out of his daydream. He pulled the gun from his waist and bolted towards Romero's house…

www.tymarshallbooks.com

www.ingramcontent.com/pod-product-compliance
Lightning Source LLC
Chambersburg PA
CBHW051920110726
47902CB00002B/355